The Man Who Wasn't There

Also by Judy Nedry

FICTION

An Unholy Alliance

The Difficult Sister

NONFICTION

Oregon Wine Country

Washington Wine Country

The Man Who Wasn't There

By Judy Nedry

This is a work of fiction. Names, characters, events, and locales are a product of the author's imagination or are used fictitiously. Any resemblance to real persons, living or dead, is entirely coincidental and not intended by the author.

Copyright 2015 by Judy Nedry and the Nedry Living Trust,
Judy Nedry, Trustee

All rights reserved. In accordance with the U.S. Copyright Act of 1976, the scanning, uploading, and electronic sharing of any part of this book without the permission of the author constitute unlawful piracy and theft of the author's intellectual property. If you would like to use material from the book (other than for review purposes), prior written permission must be obtained by contacting the author.
Thank you for your support of the author's rights.

ISBN: 978-1-68222-131-0

www.judynedry.com

BookBaby Publishing

For Wynne

> Yesterday, up on the stair,
> I met a man who wasn't there.
> He wasn't there again today,
> I wish, I wish he'd go away....
>
> – Hughes Mearns, 1899

JULY 2006
Yamhill County, Oregon

CHAPTER 1

It's difficult to enjoy oneself or anything else when it's 102 degrees, but I was giving it my best shot. I'd been invited, and I was thrilled to be mingling in the excitement, people, and the promise of delicious food. I was out of my usual milieu and I planned to enjoy myself.

I took another sip of the fancy label sparkling mineral water I'd taken from a bucket of iced beverages near my feet and wondered how the people around me could drink wine in this heat. Yet, in the old days I would have been right there with them.

Everything looked the same at the annual International Pinot Noir Celebration, except, perhaps, for the celebrants. They were all a little younger, perhaps a little more scholarly, healthier. My blurred memories were of a somewhat more debauched event, but hey, that could have been my condition at the time.

The fire pits were the same. Huge sides of salmon bound onto cedar bough racks sizzled over banked, amber coals. Nearby, a temporary bocce ball court was occupied by local and international chefs who took turns playing while they tended to the fish and other details of the upcoming feast. Occasionally one of them would throw another hunk of wood into the fire pits. Fat from the salmon dripped onto the bright coals and fragrant smoke wafted upward, filling the air with mouthwatering aromas. This was the night of the traditional Salmon Bake—an event that dazzled winemakers, chefs, wine connoisseurs, and journalists from around the world.

It's the food, rather than wine, that attracted me to this year's event. My name is Emma Golden, and I'd hung up my *tastevin* nearly eight years ago. In the years prior, I'd done some of my best work at the IPNC, which is held the last weekend in July on the Linfield College campus in McMinnville, Oregon. Standing beside my friend Cat Millet, I watched as attendees sipped some of the world's best wines and either zoned in on the chefs or mingled near the shaded wine tables. Did I miss it or not? The drinking? I guess I missed aspects of it. I missed the fun. But by the time I quit, it no longer was any fun. When alcohol quits working, the real hell begins. And in the end, alcohol had stolen my life.

I'd always had a difficult time at social events, particularly in the years before and after wine, so it was nice to have someone here with me. "Why do they do it that way?" Cat asked, gesturing toward the salmon.

We moved farther from the heat of the fire pits and I took another gulp of water while she slowly and delicately worked on a glass of chilled pinot gris. "That's how the Northwest tribes used to cook them at their feasts," I said. Wild salmon, now an endangered species on the West Coast, once had filled western rivers all the way to their headwaters. It had been the Indians' primary food source, symbol of both spirituality and prosperity. Today both the Indian and the salmon populations were severely decimated. Fish the size of those on the stakes were rare. For out-of-staters, seeing wild salmon cooked in this manner amounted to a one-of-a-kind experience.

My eyes roamed the crowd for familiar faces. I'd lived in Yamhill County for twenty years. My former husband and I raised our children here, we started a vineyard and later a winery. For many years I chronicled the Northwest wine industry in local and national publications. Then wine became my master and it was quit or die. Eight years ago I sobered up, divorced, and moved back to Portland, where I've been living ever since.

I still have a few friends out here, and one of those is Melody Wyatt. After I took issue with some of Melody's behavior last winter, I'd given her wide berth. I'd needed time to let some of the wounds from our adventure together heal. Then she called me up and offered me tickets to the IPNC Salmon Bake. Wide berth notwithstanding, I willingly took the bait. Who could resist such an offer, an opportunity to see who from my old life was doing what? I love great food, and these days I seem to eat too little of it. Melody knows all my weak spots. This really was too good to pass up. She even offered to put me and Cat up in her posh B&B, the Westerly.

Cat shoved her wine glass into my hand. "Pit stop," she said under her breath.

I pointed to a row of Honey Buckets across the lawn from the Oak Grove. "You could always fight your way to the ladies' in the Administration Building," I said. "But you'd probably have to stand in a long line."

"It's early. I'll take the Honey Buckets," she said. I watched as she began hiking across the broad lawn. Her long legs ate up the distance. Her hair, a professionally cut and highlighted bob, swayed as she walked. Little waves of heat rose from the lawn. I backed deeper into the shade and wondered how long it would stay so unbearably hot. I wiped beads of sweat from my upper lip.

A lot of people I'd known from the old days were here tonight, even if I didn't recognize most of them. In the years I'd been away from the wine business, we'd all gotten older, which for some meant big changes. A couple of my favorite friends from the past had died. I'd made it out to their funerals, but had never lingered to chat. I'd felt myself a little out of place. I no longer was involved in the food and wine scene, I no longer was practicing the craft I'd loved so much. There had been, and was tonight, the haunting discomfort I've always felt in crowds of people when not self-medicated.

I needed to pause and remind myself of the truth. I had done a hell of a job helping to make Oregon wines familiar to aficionados both within and outside the local area. God knows, it hadn't been easy, but it had been fun and worthwhile, and if anything I should at least allow myself a little pat on the back. Before I'd had to quit, I'd accomplished quite a lot. I had no reason to feel discomfort.

Eight years later, the scene had changed to a barely recognizable new reality. Rapid growth in the wine industry plus several stunning back-to-back vintages had brought media people streaming into Oregon. In this new environment, one fewer wine writer was nothing to remark upon. I hadn't been missed.

I was watching Cat as she made her way back across the lawn when I noticed man walking behind her, a big guy with hair close-cropped on his balding head and a lumbering gait like Tony Soprano. He wore a linen summer shirt and casual slacks, and he looked pretty tough. I suddenly realized I *knew* that guy!

Cat sidled up beside me, but I only noticed the man behind her. "Florian?" I called. "Florian Craig?"

The big man's head popped up. He looked in our direction. Yes, it was he. For a second he looked confused, and then he focused on me and broke into a huge smile. He bounded over to us, hand outstretched. We shook enthusiastically before he wrapped me into a bear-like hug. "What a wonderful surprise, darling! I was hoping I'd get to see you."

Florian looked like a former linebacker, but if he played any sport it would have been soccer or rugby, and that a long time ago. He hailed from England, he always looked a little shady, and he could talk like a roughneck—hilariously so. But he also cleaned up real nice, and enjoyed the distinction of being wine columnist for the *New York Times*. I'd always thought we had a lot in common— only he wrote for the *Times* and I didn't. "Bloody *hell*, it's hot!" he said as he released me. I introduced him to Cat and he reached out with his meaty paw. "Lovely to meet you, darling. Please excuse the language."

Cat shook hands and blushed. In less than thirty seconds she'd melted, and it wasn't because of the heat. Florian Craig had attracted her attention—not easy, as we women of a certain age are a somewhat jaded lot. But Florian did it so easily. It's nice to be called darling or sweetheart by someone other than a sales clerk. And no matter what else one can say about him, the man oozes a protective maleness. Had she had the same effect on him? Hard to tell. Florian was good at keeping secrets, and I couldn't discern a clue.

I hadn't seen him in ten years and I took in the look of him—tall, broad-shouldered, and thick, with a bullet-shaped head that ran straight into his shoulders. His forearms were the size of hams, he had broad hands and fingers like sausages. He was my age, give or take a couple years, and had put on a bit of weight since I'd last seen him. He was a formidable presence, and yet he moved gracefully, almost lightly, like a dancer in his large frame.

"Will you join us at dinner?" I asked. "And you're here because?"

"Keynote speaker, darling. They wanted to hear me rave about pinot noir, and I didn't disappoint. I've been following yours for some time, as you know."

"By mine do you mean my former husband's?" I wondered, referring to StoneGate, the winery owned by my ex, Dwight McCourt.

"I mean *Oregon's*, darling. The wines here are spectacular. And yes, I'd be honored to join you for the feast."

Then, just as quickly as he'd appeared, Craig glided away and melted into a group of people with an over-the-shoulder promise to find us at dinner.

"He's pretty cute," said Cat when he was out of hearing range.

She was interested. I just knew it! "He's a lot of fun," I said. "We drank together at all the wine competitions."

Cat's eyes followed Florian as he receded through clusters of people. "You must know him pretty well then?"

"Nobody knows Florian Craig very well," I told her. "Even when he's drinking, which is most of the time, it's all small talk with him. Great small talk, don't get me wrong. He knows everything about food and wine, not to mention all the players. He's dragged me kicking and screaming to several of New York's finest little-known restaurants, and I've always enjoyed his company."

Cat raised her eyebrows at me. "Strictly platonic, darling," I said, taking a stab at Craig's English accent. "Maybe *you'll* have better luck."

She laughed. "Yes, maybe I will," she said, more to herself than to me.

As the sun moved behind the Coast Range we transitioned into a hot and airless evening that was nearly as miserable as the day had been. Fairy lights strung between the trees flickered overhead. Luscious food aromas, voices, and laughter filled the air. In the center of the Oak Grove, a band began setting up. Good as his word, Florian caught up with Cat and me in time to eat. Plates loaded with grilled salmon, salads, and butter-soaked sweet corn on the cob, we staked out a table at the edge of the grove. Florian pulled three bottles of high-pedigree Burgundy out of a black canvas wine carrier, set them on the table, and commenced opening. It appeared that we were in for a perfect, albeit hot, evening.

I'd no sooner tucked into my food when a voice I'd know anywhere said, "Mind if we join you?" It was my former husband Dwight McCourt, and he was with a woman. As it turns out, it was a woman I didn't have much use for. Pamela Fontaine, aka the Bitch. I kicked Cat under the table and she took her eyes off Florian long enough to take note of the interlopers. She knew Dwight, and I'm pretty certain I'd told her about Pamela. Introductions were performed all around. Pamela and I acknowledged each other with slitty-eyed glares.

Dwight, of course, also had brought along his own secret stash of wine—a couple of StoneGate Winery's finest pinots plus a fine, aged chardonnay from a vintage I remembered well. I took another bite of salmon and surveyed the scene. It was turning out to be quite the affair. There was Dwight, almost as big as Florian, with his thick red-going-to-gray hair. He looked less rumpled than usual, and his hair and beard had been respectably trimmed. He wore slacks—a big change from his normal jeans. Then I looked at Pamela the Bitch—living proof that one can never be too rich nor too thin—with her tiny frame, expensive clothes, and expertly coiffed cap of silver hair.

Were they living together? Is that why Dwight looked so civilized? I could feel my brain racing, trying to wrap itself around that idea, all the while silently saying the Serenity Prayer. Maybe I'd get lucky and accept the things I couldn't change. Several months ago, I'd learned that Pamela had not reported her then-husband's sexual abuse of their daughter, and I'd told her in my usual tactful way what I thought about that. There'd been no love lost between us since then. I couldn't believe that someone I'd once been married to would fall for the likes of Pamela, but she's good looking and very wealthy. More to the point, the world is a very strange place.

I was getting ready to whisper something snarky in Cat's ear when someone pulled out the chair to my left. Two more bottles of wine appeared on the table. "Is this seat taken?" James Ryder, one of the founding fathers of the Oregon wine industry, stood at the table, plate in hand, expression akin to that of Oliver Twist asking for more gruel. Beside him stood his youngest daughter Stephanie.

"Sit," I ordered. James Ryder and I had been each other's biggest fans in the old days. I was delighted to see him and I knew he'd round out the table. He'd been one of my first interviews as a wine writer, and over the years had become a good friend. I knew he wasn't sitting here just to catch up with me. His motive for choosing our table to get Florian Craig's ear.

Tall and lean, with a head of thick white hair, at nearly seventy he still was very handsome. However, as with all of us, gravity would have its way. I noticed his age particularly around his eyes and neck. He leaned down and kissed me on the cheek. He absolutely reeked of booze and stale cigarette smoke.

Stephanie seated herself beside him without saying a word to anyone. She was the winemaker at Ryder Estate now, gifted in her profession but odd. Stephanie was the youngest of three daughters, and from the get-go had been inseparable from her father, even going so far as to become a winemaker in his footsteps.

While she might be a vintner extraordinaire, she didn't have a socially adept bone in her body. She'd always kept to herself when not following her dad around. Tonight she looked well beyond anti-social. Her dark blond hair hung, long and greasy, past her shoulders. A tight tank top revealed rolls of midriff and belly fat. She wore a too-short skirt and flip-flops. She looked like a train wreck and I wondered if there wasn't something going on with her—something more than simple reclusiveness.

"So good to see you, Emma," James said, his attention still focused on Florian. Once he'd parked his plate, he made his way around the table to shake hands with the rest of the group while Stephanie, expression sullen, hunched over her food and commenced shoveling it into her mouth. Once more, I leaned toward Cat. "You've met him haven't you?"

"Of course," she said. "At your place ages ago. Remember? Where's his wife?"

I watched as James made his way from person to person, pausing especially to chat with Florian Craig. He looked different. He'd gained belly weight, but more than that he sported an encroaching seediness I wasn't quite ready to acknowledge. His eyes, once always bright with adventure and mischief, had dulled. "Good question," I answered under my breath. "He's gotten a pot gut."

"Good grief, Emma! Behave yourself."

The heat must have gotten to me, not to mention being surrounded by half the wine on the planet. I had no intention of behaving myself. It struck me that something was very off with James. My mind raced and I felt a mixture of uncomfortable feelings—my feelings about him, plus those I get in large gatherings where I suddenly feel as if I'm spinning out of control. In one corner of my mind, I was back in it again, part of this life. Yet I knew that wasn't true. Irritability nagged at me leaving me feeling desperately out of place. Coming out to an event like this, with all its triggers and my own special mix of uncertainties, had been a huge mistake.

Then James was back, and seated next to me. It took only a few seconds of sitting in close proximity to realize that the man was drunk on his lips. I watched as he unsteadily and too carefully opened one of his bottles of wine. Here was the visionary who had worked hard physically and mentally to bring Ryder Estate to the top back when nobody who was anybody thought Oregon could produce decent wine. It had remained at the top because he'd continued on, relentless, to keep it there. And in the process, he'd helped to bring the rest of Oregon's once-unknown crew with him. A premier wine estate, Ryder consistently showed among the best pinot noir in the world. It didn't hurt that its owner also was a great salesman.

There had always been a fun side to James, too. I remembered the many times over the years when we'd gathered in his office for an interview and shared a bottle of wine. He'd been my pipeline, guiding me to many breaking stories about the wine industry. Now, nearing seventy, all the years of hard work and steady drinking were catching up with him. Pot gut, puffy eyes, tiny red veins on his nose and cheeks. He'd always told me he'd put quality of life over quantity any day. Watching him, I wondered how much of either he had left. He did not look like a healthy man.

I tried to suspend judgement. Any soul was entitled to a good drunk once in a while, I reasoned, and James certainly was no exception. Even drunk, he still managed that easy elegance around people. I could have been the only one at the table who noticed how impaired he was. To people who saw him regularly he probably looked just fine. Calm down, I told myself, and quit taking the world's inventory. You're not in charge. Lighten up and have some fun.

I mulled those thoughts and he opened a second bottle of wine. He poured for Florian Craig, dumped a generous amount into his own glass, and then passed the bottle down the table. Finally he was finished with his ritual. I leaned toward him. "James, it's been ages. What's going on out here that's new and dirty?"

His red face turned purple and, voice raised, he answered almost before the words were out of my mouth. "I'll tell you what's going on out here," he said, his voice a shade louder than necessary. "There's a shyster who's come up here from Las Vegas. He thinks he's going to put a destination resort up the hill from me. That little shithead is here tonight, and when I find him I'm going to straighten him out."

General conversation at our table ceased, as it did at the tables nearest ours. Obviously I was out of the loop. I lowered my voice. "Does he own the property?" I asked.

Ryder treated the table to another terse, again louder than necessary response. "Yes he does—he and a group of crooks from Nevada are trying to buy off our county commissioners, who don't have a brain among them. I don't object to a spa. The valley could use a classy resort, but why do they think they have to build it up the hill from *my* vineyard? Imagine the traffic. Think of the idiots who are going to stop their cars and walk into *my* vineyard to take a nice picture, and spread disease in the Ryder vineyards while they're at it. And what do they think they're going to do for water up there? Dig into my well?"

By now, everyone within range had stopped eating and talking. All eyes were on our table. My former husband intervened. "James," he said, as he got up and walked around the table to calm my dining partner. "This isn't really the place. How about we get together and talk this over later?"

Ryder stood, turned on him and swung a fist, which Dwight deflected easily but with a nervous laugh. Ryder stumbled, but caught himself on the back of my chair. He nearly flipped me. Florian jumped to his feet, but I managed to catch hold of the table and keep myself upright before he reached me.

James shook himself like a wet dog. He momentarily looked bewildered. "Bullshit," he said to no one in particular. "All bullshit. I'll put a stop to those crooks." He absently patted me on the shoulder, but I didn't turn around to look at him. "Just see if I don't." And with that, James Ryder grabbed his wine glass and one of his open bottles of wine from the table and marched off through the crowded tables filled with staring diners.

The rest of us looked at each other. "What just happened?" said Cat.

"He's always been passionate about his causes," I said, trying to collect myself. It was more than passion, though. It was bad craziness.

Dwight returned to his seat next to Pamela. I took another bite of the lovely salmon, but the meal had been ruined. For me it had lost its flavor. Feelings welled up in me for this man I'd so admired over the years. I'd often seen him angry, or tipsy, but never a bumbling fool.

"What was that resort stuff he was talking about?" I asked. "Is something being built out here that I don't know about?" I had been out interviewing people for a book the preceding autumn—a book that would be out in a few short months—but not a soul had mentioned a destination resort.

Dwight, who usually keeps his nose out of everybody's business, supplied the answer. "There's an outfit from Henderson, Nevada, realtors and lawyers mostly. Their front man is a guy named Max Weatherman. He's a lawyer, and he's gotten into some trouble with the law down in Henderson regarding some of his properties. So now he and his company are up here investing in real estate. I saw him here tonight." Then he looked in the direction James had headed. "Oh, shit. I hope James doesn't find him."

"Yes, but what about the resort?" I prodded.

Dwight shot me a look. "The plan is for a destination resort—hotel, spa, restaurant, the works—up the hill behind Ryder's property. Ryder doesn't want it on principle, but everybody in Yamhill County knows there's no water up there."

"Why can't they just put it in the valley?"

"Obviously, these developer folks think it would be romantic"—Dwight made quote marks with his fingers while Pamela managed to look bored—"to have the thing up on a hillside with a view of the valley and the mountains, overlooking vineyards, et cetera. They are pushing the county hard about how building it will create jobs, tourism, economic growth, the usual stuff."

"Which translates into wrecking the landscape and adding a bunch of minimum wage jobs," I said. "No wonder he's angry."

I was about to really get on my soapbox when yelling erupted several tables away. From the sound of it, James Ryder had located Max Weatherman and was about to "straighten him out". Automatically, several of us jumped to our feet and dashed in the direction of the noise.

When we closed in on the fracas and could see what it was all about, I drew in my breath sharply. James and a somewhat younger man stood about five feet apart, face-to-face, like two roosters waiting to be loosed so they could kill each other.

Once again, James Ryder's complexion had turned an unhealthy shade of purple. A shank of his perfect white hair had fallen into his face. The other man, whom I assumed to be Max Weatherman, appeared to be red with anger as well, but it could have been his fake tan, which gave him an overall orange cast. He was shorter than James, and trim. His razor-cut, sandy blond hair stuck to his forehead. He tried to look calm, but sweat dribbled in little rivulets down his face and his bright Hawaiian shirt clung to his torso, announcing to one and all that he was anything but serene. He appeared to be early fifties, and he wore a big gold chain around his neck.

What was James thinking to get himself into such a tawdry situation? It was none of my business, of course, and he didn't seem the least bit concerned to be making an ass of himself. "You son of a bitch!" he screamed at Weatherman, voice cracking. He was beyond drunk, he was insane.

Weatherman, to his credit, stepped back and held his hands out in what appeared to be a calming gesture. "James, relax," he said. "There's no need for the bad language."

James wasn't having it. "Don't make nice with me." He took a step toward Weatherman, who took a step backward to keep some distance between them. "You're no good, Weatherman. You are up here to exploit us and make trouble, and I won't have it."

Weatherman pulled a feigned expression of deep hurt. He seemed, in his own peculiar way, to be taunting his adversary. "I don't know what you're talking about, James. I am up here doing business and trying to breathe some life into this otherwise lifeless economy."

I stood frozen, taking it all in. "Our economy is doing just fine without the likes of you, Weatherman." James's voice boomed, and then it dropped to a menacing tone so that I had difficulty hearing him. "Go back to Nevada where they appreciate the way you do business. We don't want the mafia involved in our industry. I know all about you, what you did, and why you moved up here with your tail between your legs. I've done my research on you. You won't get away with that Las Vegas bullshit here in Oregon." Then the once-elegant James Ryder took another step toward Weatherman and made a quick and unexpected upper cut to his chin. It barely touched him. All around me I heard a huge, collective gasp.

In response, Weatherman lashed up and out with his right fist. Pop! It landed solidly on Ryder's purple nose. The next thing I knew, the two men were rolling on the ground punching, kicking, snorting, and grunting, to surrounding cries of shock and horror. The fisticuffs quickly ended when several men dived into the melee and separated the fighters.

Weatherman scrambled to his feet, his nose bloodied and two buttons missing from his Tommy Bahama shirt. He dusted himself off, spat onto the ground, turned and walked more-or-less calmly in the direction of the portable toilets.

James, meanwhile, had crawled to his hands and knees, where he stayed for several long seconds before being helped to his feet.

He shook his head as if he wasn't sure what hit him, and looked around. Those surrounding him, myself included, watched with a combination of shock and pity. What a mess. Still in a state of disbelief, I glanced. Cat was standing near me. I grabbed her by the arm and we stood there clutching each other. "What the *hell*? she said.

"This is just ridiculous," I replied. "I can't believe he'd stoop to that level of behavior."

Someone wanted to call the police. Someone else said, "No, we don't need any more trouble. It's over." James's nose bled profusely. He staunched it with a white handkerchief. Despite the fact that he couldn't stand without lurching back and forth, he still felt feisty. "I'll get you," he yelled hoarsely at Weatherman's vanishing back. "I won't forget this. You'll pay for this!"

People slowly dropped away from him. He looked around drunkenly, a little lost. I marched over to him and stuck my face in front of his. "Shut up, James," I said, not caring who heard me. "You're too old for this crap. And you need to do something about that nose."

He reached up, grasped his nose, and adjusted it slightly. I heard the crunch of cartilage and recoiled. James treated me to an off-kilter grin while his nose began to bleed with renewed vigor. He was too inebriated to feel any pain. He re-applied the bloody handkerchief, and held everything together for several seconds. "I'll be fine," he said when the bleeding finally subsided. "This old nose has been broken before and nobody died."

I sighed in disgust. "Do it your way, then, you damned old fool. I'll leave you to it. Why isn't Lila here to keep you out of trouble?"

Ryder stood there for a moment as if thinking how to reply. "She's not well," he said. After a pause, he added, "The cancer is back."

It hit me like a punch in the gut. "I am so sorry," I said. No wonder he was behaving so badly. Anger is the first line of defense for people who don't know how to deal with their emotions. "You need to get home to her."

His eyes wandered away from me and he took another dab at his rapidly swelling nose. "Yes, I suppose I do," he said. He pushed his hair back with a bloodied hand, leaving a streak across his forehead.

I kissed him on the cheek. I now felt more sadness for him than anger. "Goodnight, James. Get Stephanie to take you home, and I'll come by tomorrow to see Lila."

"She'd like that," he said. Then, with a simple nod at me and Cat, he took his leave.

Back at our table, the ranks had increased. News of Florian Craig's whereabouts had reached a number of winemakers. People I'd never seen before had pulled up chairs and set their best wine offerings on the table hoping to be noticed. Florian was happy to be in the center of things, tasting wines and then spitting them into a bucket.

I spotted Melody advancing upon us with a basket filled with yet more wine. So that's how she was spending her volunteer time. Melody is one of my oldest friends. We raised our children together and drank together in the old days. Melody never drank like me and our late friend Caroline, but she sure knew how to have fun. Back in the day, when we went into Portland together for a night on the town, we dubbed ourselves Stella, Ruby, and Viola. That way, if one of us got into minor trouble, nobody knew our real names. Caroline was Stella, I was Ruby, and Melody, of course, was Viola.

Melody loved to make fashion statements. Tonight she was outfitted as Carmen Miranda with a puffy sleeved white peasant blouse and a big poufy skirt that could have doubled as a tablecloth. A straw hat topped with large pieces of plastic fruit completed the ensemble. Ridiculous but fun, and she pulled it off. Crowds parted and heads turned as she moved toward us. Even under all that skirt you could see her hips rolling seductively. Her makeup was perfect, as was her dark, wavy, silver-shot hair. Her brilliant red lips were parted revealing sparkling white teeth. Though I have observed her for years, I still manage to get caught up in her performance art.

"How y'all doing here?" she asked, affecting her departed mother's West Texas drawl. She surveyed the table. "Anybody *need* anything?" She put her arm around Dwight—they'd always been buddies, plus she knew how much it would bother Pamela the Bitch. There was no love lost between the two of them, either. In fact, Melody was the one responsible for Pamela's moniker well before she and Dwight were an item. Pamela had always treated Melody like she was a hayseed, and Melody was "real good at getting even."

While Pamela fumed, the others sorted through Melody's wine offerings and managed to unearth another treasure or two. I stood up and looked over the table. Several more folks were sidling up with their chairs and glasses, hoping for an audience with Mr. *New York Times*. It was going to be a long evening, but not for me.

"Happy trails," I said, to nobody in particular. Florian noticed me and looked up. He waved a pinky at me and winked. Cat stood up as if to leave. "Stay here," I told her. I could hear the band rocking the oldies behind us. "The evening's young. You might get a chance to dance, and Florian can give you a ride back. He's staying at the Westerly." She grinned at me and sat back down.

Every recovering drunk who hopes to remain sober has an escape plan. I'd known going into this party that, if I suddenly had to disappear, Cat could ride home with Melody. The reason I'd been offered tickets in the first place was because she was volunteering for the Salmon Bake food committee. Normally she and her husband Dan volunteered together, but this year he was fishing in Alaska. Melody would be here late, until after things shut down. But then along came Florian. I smiled to myself.

But I was done for the night. First, there'd been all that exposure to Dwight and Pamela. Not that I wanted him back, I told myself. But couldn't he have found someone *nice*? And then James—to see him falling apart and to witness his behavior had been unpleasant to say the least. I was worried about the old bird. And Lila? As if I didn't know what cancer coming back could mean? She had a rough road ahead. She'd never been my best friend, or even close to it. But our paths crossed often when I lived in Yamhill County. I knew she would need a lot of support in the upcoming months and I hoped I could find a way to step up and offer at least some assistance.

I made my way toward my car, stopping briefly to dig a tissue out of my handbag. I was sweaty and my face was sticky, a fact I hadn't noticed until that moment. I dabbed at my face with the tissue. The evening still clung to the day's heat, but it had cooled somewhat. The sun had set and the western sky glowed deep purple. Once off the valley floor, it would be a pleasant drive up the hill to the Westerly and my air-conditioned room.

The Honey Buckets loomed ahead of me in the falling dusk. As much as I hate those things, I also realized once I relaxed and caught my breath, that I needed one. It was nearly dark, and the fairy lights hadn't made it this far from the Oak Grove. Fortunately, I only needed to reach into my bag for that tiny flashlight I always carry. At least I'd know up front if the toilets were really gross. In that likely event, there was a nice stand of bushes behind them that might prove useful.

I shined my little light on the doors. In use. In use. In use. Vacant. The empty one beckoned me, but my eyes flicked to the bank of shrubs behind it. For some reason I have had a lifelong phobia about dark, empty public restrooms.

I looked around again. At the far end of the bank of latrines a man approached. By this time, I'd gotten myself pretty worked up at the thought of entering one of them. But since lots of folks like that man were wandering around out here in the twilight with me, the bushes probably weren't such a great idea.

Time to man up, I told myself. I grabbed the handle and twisted it with one hand, flashlight at the ready in the other. At first the door wouldn't open. I shook it a little without pulling it open, in case someone had forgotten to lock it. "Anybody in there?" I said, and stepped back. The door burst open. A huge figure jumped out of the Honey Bucket and onto me. I fell backward, but not before managing one very loud scream as we both crumpled into a heap on the ground.

CHAPTER 2

Someone was on top of me, crushing me! I screamed again, this time gagging on my own fear. "Fire! Fire!" I rasped. It was as if the sounds wouldn't come out of me. I was in complete panic mode, afraid I wouldn't be heard. I'd read somewhere that no one responded to "Help!" anymore, and I was certain this guy meant to kill me. I kicked, wiggled, and struggled. I gasped and squawked. Two people began to pull him off me. Then finally I got my voice back. "Don't let him get away!" I cried. "Hold on to him. He attacked me!" More people ran to help us.

I rolled over and scrambled to my feet, completely disoriented, scared, and angry as hell. I trembled all over. My legs felt like rubber. My assailant lay motionless on the ground. People shoved their way in, temporarily blocking my view. "Oh my God, he's hurt," said one of the women. I looked wildly about me. I didn't think I could have hurt him much. Where was that flashlight? My right hand touched my chest and I realized that the front of my brand new sundress was soaked through. During the commotion, I'd become separated from my handbag.

I heard a man's voice. "He's all bloody. Someone find a doctor fast!" I clutched the front of my dress and pulled away my wet hand. It was dark and sticky, and suddenly everything switched to slow motion. I realized what I'd smelled, besides the booze and sweat, was blood. Oozy, sticky blood. I wiped my hands on my skirt. Then I picked up the skirt hem and rubbed my hands slowly but determinedly, as if I were Lady Macbeth fixated on the damned spot. All the time, my back was turned to the person on the ground.

More people advanced upon the scene, drawn by the hubbub. None of them gave me as much as a glance. Voices rose and fell. A wave of nausea passed through me. I mustered the courage to turn around and look through the gathered horde. There on the ground a scant ten feet away lay James Ryder. Even in the near darkness I could see he was drenched in blood. A handle of some sort protruded from beneath his rib cage, its awkward angle adding to the surreal quality of the sight. He looked pretty dead to me. His mouth gaped wide open, his eyes were dull and unfocused. I wanted to feel something, to cry out, but I couldn't. I was paralyzed. What on earth had happened?

People hovered close to him, but I couldn't move. I stood frozen, staring at my old friend's body. No thoughts came, as if my brain had turned to mush. It was as if I wasn't there, wasn't a part of it in any way. And yet I was.

Suddenly Cat was by my side. I turned to face her, and her eyes registered amazement. "What's going on?" she asked. "Oh dear God, look at you!"

My mouth was so dry I could barely speak. I sucked in a big breath and said, "Something awful just happened, Cat. James is dead. I think he's been stabbed."

Cat's mouth dropped open. She looked around us, then back at me. "It can't be him," she said. "He was just at our table. Wasn't he?" Her voice was flat, testing the words, unsure. And then she looked me up and down again. "And look at you. Your dress is ruined. What did you do?"

As my mind processed what had happened I found it difficult to keep my voice steady. I gulped for air. "He left after the fight, remember? He was in the porta-potty. When I opened the unlocked the door, he fell out on top of me. I thought I was being attacked. I hit him and kicked him. And there's all this blood." A sob welled up and I tried to stop it. My body shook. I covered my face with my hands.

Cat put her arm around me and pulled me to her. "My poor friend, I'm so sorry." She rubbed between my shoulders and I found myself blubbering. "And poor James. Your poor friend James. How in the world could something like this happen?"

I sniffed. I heard siren noise, and it was getting closer. Cat handed me a tissue. "Thanks," I said. "I don't know. It looks as if he's been stabbed." I was repeating myself, but I kept talking. "The police are coming. They'll be here in a minute, and they'll know what to do. If he was murdered, they're going to want statements from everybody. We'll be here all night. *All of us!* And it will be ghastly. You don't know how often I've hoped and prayed I'd never, ever have to go through something like this again."

"You need to stop," said Cat. "This isn't helping, so stop with it before the police get here. I know this has been a horrible shock, but you need to pull yourself together, because just to look at you, the first thing they're going to think is that you stabbed him. So breathe, dammit. *Breathe.*"

She was right. There I was covered with blood. I knew him. We'd been close friends. People usually know their murderers. We'd been sitting at a table together. We'd been talking. Then he got in that fight. He'd behaved badly and I'd wanted to slap some sense into him. I sucked in and exhaled a couple of huge breaths. My body shook as we stood there and watched and waited with everyone else. My knees were so wobbly I finally couldn't stand, so I just sat on the ground. Cat rummaged around among the dozens of legs and feet and located my handbag. She brought it to me and sat on the lawn beside me.

The fire engine and ambulance arrived first. They pulled up on the side street behind the Honey Buckets and bushes. Fire fighters and EMTs raced toward us with big lights, their carriers filled with lifesaving equipment. Two of them pulled on surgical gloves and kneeled by the body while others moved the crowd far enough back that they could perform their tasks. As we stood and backed away, I heard them talking to each other, but it sounded like gibberish. The people who had gathered were not eager to be moved. They moved in slow motion but spoke in excited gibberish too. They'd showed up, so now it was their tragedy, too.

Then the police arrived. They came from all directions, some running while the older, fatter ones walked as quickly as they could. Cat and I bunched together watching as law enforcement officers gathered around the body. Then several began securing the crime scene. One stayed close, watching the paramedics, asking questions and taking notes while the others fanned out, as if following a script, to do their jobs.

"Who found him?" boomed one of the bulky officers to the assembled crowd. I stepped forward. "You?" he said. I nodded. "Did you know the deceased?" He shined his flashlight on me.

I felt as if I was standing on a stage, as if all the lights were on me and I didn't know my lines. "I do," I said. "I did. Yes." Then I started crying again.

The cop muttered something over his shoulder to one of his underlings, then refocused his attention on me. The younger man he'd addressed came to stand beside him, notebook at the ready. The older cop moved closer to me. He was about fifty, pock-marked, big-boned but not fat. "What is your name, ma'am, and how were you acquainted with the deceased?"

I could sense Cat hovering nearby; she had my back. "I'm Emma Golden. This is James Ryder. He and I were old friends in the wine business."

He shifted his weight. I could tell that something shifted in his mind as well. "How did you get that blood all over you? Did you come out here to meet him?"

"No sir. I came out here to go to the bathroom." Something that still hadn't been attended to, by the bye. "He fell out of the toilet onto me."

He walked up closer to me—so close I could smell his rancid breath—and looked at me in my blood-soaked dress. He was right in my face. From his expression, I knew I looked pretty wild. His proximity made me uncomfortable. I took a step backward. "A likely story. How much have you had to drink?" he asked.

The question seemed designed to make me nervous, and it did. I put my hand to my soggy chest. "What? I, er…uh…nothing. I don't drink."

The officer looked as if he'd arrived at a decision. "At the Pinot Noir Celebration and she doesn't drink?" he said to his sidekick. "We'll see about that." Then to me he said, "Did you kill Mr. Ryder?"

I panicked. "No," I said. To me, my voice sounded hysterical. Calm down, *calm down*. "No, I didn't kill him. He was my friend."

Again, I got the once over, the bad cop look. Nice. "You're going to have to answer some more questions, so stick around." He walked away.

I looked around desperately. This was not my life. And James Ryder wasn't really dead. It was worse than a nightmare. A low moan escaped me.

"Bloody hell!" said a voice behind us. "What's going on here?" Florian Craig had arrived on the scene. He barged through the crowd of people and had himself a good look at the dead man. He studied the scene for probably thirty seconds, then came back and stood next to us. "What? Caught him in the loo? One little shove up under the rib cage and into the aorta." He looked me up and down. "And just look at you, sweetheart. Were you in there with him? Or are you the murderer?"

Cat glared at him. "Not funny!"

Florian looked momentarily contrite, and then walked over to have another look. He took in the outhouses and where James lay relative to them. After a couple minutes he was back beside us. "That's an odd angle to the body," he observed.

"It's been moved," I said. "First he fell out on top of me, then I kicked and screamed and some people came over and pulled him off me. The whole scene is messed up."

Florian rubbed the bristles on his scalp and looked around some more. "Was anybody out here with you?"

I scrunched my face trying to remember the scene immediately before I opened that door.

"No. I was on my way back to the Westerly," I said. "It was pretty quiet. I was walking to my car trying to decide whether to stop here or go in the bushes. Then a man came along to use the toilet and I didn't want to get caught—"

"—in the bushes with your knickers down. Bad form, that." Florian chuckled, but it was without humor. "And you didn't see anyone else out here, darling?"

"No, I told you." Emotions flooded me again. My voice trembled. "I just wanted to go back to the Westerly, and instead *this* happened." I had been lingering very close to tears, and now they started running down my face again, this time in earnest.

Florian came closer and gave me a little squeeze from the side so he wouldn't get bloody. "Not to worry, darling. We're going to get this sussed."

We? What the hell did that mean? There was no 'we' about it. The big boys were going to sort out this one, and that was that. And I would be as far away as possible, or at least back in Lower Hillsdale Heights where I belonged. Unless they decided to throw me in jail. I'd learned enough to know that murderers are dangerous. They're crazy. They're narcissistic. They usually carry lethal weapons of some sort. So, no, thank you very much.

I did not voice my opinions aloud. Florian could live out his little fantasy of justice being done—it just wouldn't have anything to do me. He probably was blowing hot air, but he appeared to be uncannily comfortable with the crime scene, which reminded me of all the things I didn't know about him and his pre-wine writing existence. Maybe encouraging him and Cat wasn't such a great idea after all. I wouldn't want to put her in harm's way.

Then I had another thought. Where was Max Weatherman? I scanned the people in our immediate vicinity. Nary a sign of him, but the last time I'd seen him he was headed in the direction of what was now a crime scene. Then I noted the absence of another person who should have been there. Stephanie Ryder, who'd been glued to her dad for most of the evening. Was it possible she'd left the event, slipped away before I did, and now was somewhere, possibly home, completely unaware of the horror? She could have done so, and easily. She was not the sort of person we'd miss.

We watched the proceedings with interest. A little canopy had been erected in haste. It had drop-down sides so we no longer had to look at the body. The police also had installed a hasty barrier with stakes and yellow police line tape. It seemed to cover a very large area, but who knew where a clue may turn up? Armed with heavy duty flashlights, other members of the law enforcement team carefully combed through the bushes and over the grounds for evidence. More people were lining up along the barrier to watch the action.

We had nothing better to do but observe. Those of us who'd been on the scene had to stay put until someone in authority released us. I found the action fascinating—infinitely more so than watching a bunch of people get drunk on superb wines I'd never get to taste again. It temporarily separated me from the shock and horror of the murder. Meanwhile, nobody was going to be using those Honey Buckets any time soon. Finally, the police circulated and culled out those they didn't want to talk with. About a dozen of us remained for questioning.

CHAPTER 3

It was nearly midnight when I drove up the Westerly's long drive and parked in my usual spot at the back of the huge Prairie Foursquare house. I'd been questioned and re-questioned. I'd been badgered by that unpleasant pock-marked officer, who practically accused me of the murder. I'd probably still be there, or in jail, but sheriff's detectives Haymore and Jeffers showed up in the middle of the proceedings. Of course, I had to go through it all again with them, but at least we knew each other well enough that they realized I most likely wasn't a murderer.

I'd met the two of them the previous autumn during what was now referred to as the Cougar Crossing murders involving a prominent and unpopular winery owner and his family. They knew my story. They talked the grouchy police officer out of booking me, allowing me to return to the Westerly. They said they'd be in touch. I knew they'd make good on their promise.

I walked around the deck, planning to enter unobtrusively through the kitchen, and was surprised to find a welcoming party. Melody was hosting nightcaps on the deck. An expensive bottle of scotch sat by Florian Craig's elbow and he smoked one of Dan's contraband Cuban cigars. Cat and Melody nursed glasses of iced tea. The mood was somber.

Melody's eyes popped when she saw me covered in drying blood. She almost said something, but I was too quick for her. "I'll have what you're having," I said, then made my way up to my room to strip off my blood-encrusted clothes. I threw on a robe, and, not caring what I looked like, came back downstairs. I carried my bundle of ruined clothes with me and deposited the wad into the trash receptacle near the deck. Meanwhile, Melody had brought a frosted pitcher of iced tea and another glass out onto the deck. She filled the glass and handed it to me, topped hers and Cat's, and sat down.

I plopped into an empty chair and gulped down about half of the tea. "So what are we doing?" I asked, setting my glass on the table. "Did I miss anything?"

"Oh, no," said Melody. "We were just cussin' and *dis*-cussin'. Poor old James. I sure didn't see his end coming in quite that way."

"He could be an ornery old sod, but I always believed it was mostly an act," said Florian. "Great guy. Told it like it was." He took a judicious sip of his scotch and then stared morosely into his glass. "I'm going to miss him. He'd call me every week or two—whenever he had a particularly good joke." He chuckled to himself.

"Yeah, his jokes were the best," I said. And then my eyes started running again. "The orneriest guy around, but people loved him. So who could have done such a thing?"

Florian took another sip of scotch. "Like I said earlier, sweetheart, we'll figure it out."

"No *we* won't, Florian. I'm not having anything to do with this."

And then Melody popped in. "But Emma, you're so good at this."

I bristled. "Don't even go there, Melody."

"Emma…."

"*No!*" I said. "I got stuck in your adventure last winter and it turned out horribly. Besides, Florian didn't mean we in the *we* sense, did you Florian?"

Cat's eyes had bounced back and forth between us like she was following a ping pong ball. Now she fixed them on Florian. "Actually, sweetheart, I was just thinking we might have a go at it," he said.

I sat there staring at him. Finally I said, "You. Can't. Be. Serious."

"You notice things, darling."

"We all notice things. There are people who are *trained* to notice the kinds of things you're talking about. I'm not one of them."

This was out of hand. They'd all had too much to drink. As it was my only choice, I switched gears completely. I said, "James told me Lila's cancer has come back. He was headed home to look after her after that fracas with Weatherman."

In a gesture I knew too well, Melody's hand went straight to her heart. "I had no *idea* anything was wrong with Lila. None. Although she wasn't drinking wine when we had them over a couple weeks ago. She said it had something to do with her medication."

For a couple minutes nobody said anything. "I wonder if James was much of a help to her," I said, ending the period of silence.

Melody, as usual, was quick with an opinion. "Oh, you know him, Emma. He was usually pretty caught up in his own stuff. I wouldn't want him waitin' on me."

Of course. The big ego. I was very familiar with that aspect of James's personality. "Well, I'd sure like to know who did this," I said. "That grouchy cop who interviewed me acts like he thinks I did it. Talk about rotten timing."

"I'd be more interested in that Max Weatherman bloke if it were me asking the questions," said Florian. "He's up to no good, that one."

I'd had passing thoughts about Weatherman as well. "Funny, I didn't see him after all this went down," I said.

"I saw him earlier this evening," said Florian. "He had himself wrapped around a leggy brunette bit of fluff about half his age."

The old sleaze. However, in my mind this cleared Weatherman from any wrongdoing. In general, men tend not to multi-task well. I'd never known of a man who was trying to get a woman in bed to push the pause button and go do something else—say, run to the grocery store or murder someone. Even if Weatherman was the guy who would make an exception to the rule, it was a long shot at best. "Was that before or after his fight with James?"

"It was after," Melody said. "It looked like they were going somewhere. Since he had his hand on her butt, it didn't appear he had murder on his mind, or that he even noticed there'd been one." Then she shifted her attention to me. "Too bad about your frock."

I shrugged in my bathrobe. With so many thoughts racing through my mind, I'd forgotten all about it. "Yes. I bought it special for today, and now it's in the trash." I stood up, refilled my tea glass, and for the second time that evening prepared to take my leave. "You'll have to excuse me. It's been a long day."

Florian filled his glass with more scotch, then raised it to me. "You've had quite the evening, darling. Sleep well." Melody and Cat said goodnight and then put their heads close together and started talking. It looked as if they would be at it all night. Which was fine with me.

I entered the kitchen, which is approximately the size of my entire living quarters. For all the quaintness of the painted wood, glass-fronted cabinets, and an old oak butcher block, this room was anything but quaint when it came to equipment. At the far end, near the sliders to the deck, were doors that led to a separate laundry room and a mud room, and a walk-in pantry that housed a commercial refrigerator. The main kitchen area boasted a six-burner commercial gas range with two ovens, next to it a separate built-in convection oven. There were large stainless steel sinks, a separate wet bar, a salad prep area, and a baking station complete with a polished concrete slab. Pots and pans hung from ceiling hooks; ceramic serving platters and bowls were stacked neatly on baker's racks against one wall. The place was outfitted better than many restaurants.

I crossed the room, past the alcove where Melody's messy antique oak desk sat, and opened the door of what appeared to be a broom closet, but actually housed the little stairway that led up to my private suite—the one Melody had installed in a former attic space when she'd added onto and remodeled the Westerly's kitchen the previous year. It was a large and beautifully appointed room with *en suite* bath complete with a soaking tub and a walk-in shower. I headed straight for the shower.

There I heaved a great sigh, turned on the water, and adjusted the shower head so that hot water pelleted my body like hail.

Initially the water was a grotesque pink as it rolled off me. I soaped myself liberally, scrubbed everywhere, shampooed and conditioned, and watched until everything ran clear. Then I just stood there for several minutes, allowing myself to be pummeled by the steaming water until I couldn't stand it anymore and I finally felt cleansed. I toweled my hair and ran a comb through it. It would be dry before lights out.

I turned off the air conditioning and popped open a window to let in the fresh night air. Then I crawled into bed with my trusty spiral notebook and a pen. I was ready to process and let myself get lost in the evening's events. I sipped a little of the iced tea and took another deep breath. The sheets felt cool and welcoming. I plumped a couple of fat pillows behind my back, and commenced scribbling in the notebook—an activity that has served me well since I returned to this practice the previous October when I stayed in my beautiful room here at the Westerly for six weeks.

Maybe life has gotten more complicated over the past several years; maybe it's just age. Whatever it is, I've discovered in recent months what a comfort it is to put certain thoughts and events in writing. It's like talking to a trusted friend, only I have a record rather than just the portion of the conversation my brain chooses to remember.

I began by writing about James's death. It had so traumatized me that I still felt wooden, numb, and yet I couldn't not write about it. All the blood. There had been so much blood! Every time I closed my eyes I saw it all over again. I saw every scene from the evening just past. I felt blown apart, in shock from the horrible event, and I knew there were emotions down there somewhere waiting to bubble up and blindside me when I least expected them. But for now all I could think about was what I'd seen.

The second I'd pounded on that door with the little green vacant tab, the world had turned upside down. First came the terror, the feeling of being attacked that had overwhelmed me and turned me into a panicked, squealing fool. How unnerving to unravel so quickly, but I'd been caught completely off guard. And then to see my old friend lying there dead. It was impossible to fathom. We'd been good friends for so long—nearly three decades. At times we'd been confidants. So many conversations, so many memories. I began channeling onto the page beneath my hand how just deep had been my friendship with him.

James had been one of the stories behind the story of the Oregon wine industry. Along with a half dozen others who had moved to western Oregon in the late 1960s and early 1970s specifically to raise European wine grapes and make wine, James had been tough, scrappy, smart, in-your-face, and resourceful. It just went with the territory. The people who started this industry had guts and moxie, and James had been one of the leaders of the pack. It was one of the reasons I'd always admired him. Sure, he was rough around the edges, but for some reason he had befriended me.

After that tenuous first interview, when he challenged me and took stock of the green female wine journalist who sat before him, we'd formed an alliance. And his wicked sense of humor! How I'd enjoyed his damn-the-torpedoes views of life and the business over the years. Yet I knew he gave everything he had to making his winery, and others in the area, successful. Now he was gone. I couldn't imagine the Oregon wine industry without him.

We all knew the industry had changed. I hadn't realized how much until my six weeks at the Westerly last fall. When James and Lila had come to the Willamette Valley to grow wine grapes, it was possible for ordinary people to start a vineyard. The land had been cheap. People like us lived in the little run-down farmhouses on the property. We didn't have a lot, but we somehow made it work.

More recently, the wine industry had transformed from the early days band of committed souls who lived modestly and worked hard to prove what could be done here into a big money game. The money people lived well. They didn't muck in the dirt. They didn't start their wineries in the garage or the pole barn. They didn't make the wine and hope someone would buy it. They built wineries and mansions and hired winemakers and vineyard managers with master's degrees in viticulture and enology, and then they hired branding specialists. These were businesses for them, but not the businesses that had made their fortunes. I'd heard a long time ago that the way to make a small fortune in the wine business is to start with a large one. The newcomers to Oregon wine country already had made their large fortunes elsewhere. That's what it took to get started here these days.

Change was inevitable, particularly when Oregon wines began living up to their potential. On the plus side, it wasn't easy to find a bad bottle of Oregon wine anymore. The minus? Well, it didn't feel down-home anymore. I didn't feel the passion was there as it had been in the past. Because it was a business to them rather than a lifestyle, the new people seemed a bit more distant from their land.

As usually happens in any successful endeavor, the wine industry had outgrown its roots. People James's age had retired, or were on the verge of retiring. If their children didn't want to participate in the industry, wineries were sold. I'd been a part of the early days. I'd been eager to tell the story. Dwight and I eventually had started our own winery—before the price got too high. It had been fun. Less so now. It was still good, just different. For me it was the past, a memory, and now, James with it.

But who would kill him? I wondered, and was distressed by the wondering. My mind fixated on the one person who probably would find himself on the suspect list—Max Weatherman. I knew nothing about the man, except that he had a plan that violated Oregon's land use laws and was trying to get around them, and that he had punched James in the nose. James had asked for it. But killing? This guy looked like a cool, bloodless type of person. Further, he looked like the type who'd be more concerned with getting blood on his expensive loafers than someone who'd commit a gruesome murder. Murder elevated a land-use dispute to a totally different level that in this case, to me at least, made no sense.

Despite his passionate opposition, James really didn't have any say over whether the spa would be allowed or not. Weatherman knew that. Thus, except for sheer craziness on Weatherman's part, it eliminated the motive. James had started the fracas; Weatherman had gotten fed up and popped him on the nose to shut him up. It was that simple. In his place, I would have punched him too. But what about that "mafia" word? Did Weatherman really have acquaintances or business associates so undesirable? I'd have to look into that one.

Oops! Don't go there. That is exactly what I *wouldn't* be doing, and I had my reasons.

Everyone had enemies. Someone as outspoken as James undoubtedly had lots of people who didn't like him for one reason or another. But in the wine industry he was generally well thought of and respected. Journalists loved him because in addition to his passion, he was never at a loss for the pithy quote—the type we all love to pass on to our readers. It was possible that he had wronged someone so egregiously to cause that person to do murder. I couldn't imagine what kind of offense he'd have committed. But someone had a huge resentment—unless, of course, the murderer had accidentally gotten the wrong person out there in the dark. That also was something to ponder.

I paused in my writing and took a sip of the now room-temperature tea. I could feel myself fading after a long, hot, stressful day and evening. The night had cooled off nicely and a pleasant breeze wafted through the open window. It seemed weird to be back in this room that had been home for so long the previous autumn. My friendship with Melody had been a bit tenuous since last winter when she had pulled what, in my opinion, was some truly vile behavior. Not that I've ever been a poster child for best-behaved person in the room. When she called a week ago to lure me out here, I knew she'd wanted to mend fences, but she'd made it sound like no big deal.

"Emma, you've just *got* to come out this weekend," she'd said to me without preamble, as if I was a frequent visitor, which I'm not. "It's too hot for you to be sitting around in the city. I've got two tickets to the Salmon Bake and Dan and I can't use them. Dan's gone to Alaska fishing and I'm doing my usual volunteering with the food committee."

Then she'd broken into my thoughts with, "You can bring a friend…if there's some *man* you've got your eye on."

Not that again, I thought. "There is no man. I'll bring along Cat," I told her, meaning I'd already decided to accept. I was ready to be out of Portland for a bit, and away from the redundant routine of my life. So ready, in fact, that I'd hurried down to my favorite neighborhood boutique and purchased a new sundress to commemorate the occasion. My poor dress!

Tonight I again was luxuriating at the Westerly. Cat was off in another wing of the house in her own beautiful room. We'd head back to the city tomorrow, but not before I'd taken the time to pay my respects to James's widow.

Absolutely exhausted, I closed my notebook, stowed it, and turned off the lamp on the bedside table. At last I was too tired to think any more about James's horrible death. I was just snuggling down into that comfy bed when something landed with a solid thump on the foot of it in the dark. Winston, Melody's Standard Schnauzer, had found his way up the stairway. He turned around several times and then flopped next to me on the bed. I patted him on the head. "Good boy," I said, and quickly drifted into sleep—but not before

I heard the deep, throaty growl of a sports car as it passed beneath my window.

CHAPTER 4

"He's slick as a mole," Melody said. "And, like a mole, he's always popping up where he's least wanted."

We were sitting around the old oak dining table in her kitchen drinking our first cups of coffee, and had been admiring the flowers outside on the deck before the subject of Max Weatherman came up. It was seven—early. Winston had sneaked down the stairs before I awakened. I figured our little trysts were nobody's business but our own.

Angel Lopez, the Westerly's superb *chef de cuisine*, sat at the table with us. She's not a trained chef, but the woman cooks like Escoffier. Melody had mentioned that Max Weatherman, subject of last night's controversy, was staying in the Carriage House. While Melody welcomed all kinds of guests to the Westerly and treated them equally well, it didn't necessarily follow that she liked them all.

She'd filled me in on the details of Weatherman's efforts to coerce the county commissioners into granting him a land-use variance of some kind so he could build his hilltop spa in an area designated forty-acre-minimum agricultural by the State of Oregon. She found his behavior despicable. "Given the laws of the land," she informed us, "it's very doubtful he'll get that thing approved where he wants it."

The roar of a sports car engine caused me to look outside in time to see a silver BMW 2006 Z4 pull up next to the deck. Within seconds, the maligned Mr. Weatherman appeared on the deck in all his fake-and-bake tanned glory. The only thing separating us was a screen. Melody opened it and he stepped into the kitchen.

I took full advantage of this opportunity to have a better look. His sandy blond hair was thinning and going to gray. He was wonderfully turned out in another Tommy Bahama summer shirt, crisp khaki trousers, and boating shoes with no socks. In the old days I would have been impressed. Today, a big neon sign lodged somewhere in my jaded brain flashed "egomaniac". Or it may have flashed "peckerhead". I'm not sure. I had not yet consumed the proper amount of caffeine and my mind wasn't working properly. And I really had no quarrel with him, did I? Unless he was the low-down scum bag who'd murdered my friend. To me, that still didn't seem likely. Too prissy.

"Sorry about the bother," he said. "A light burned out in my bathroom."

Melody gave him a quick once-over and something adversarial passed between them. "Thanks for letting me know. We'll take care of it." Her voice was calm, casual. "Will you be joining us for breakfast? I could send someone out if you'd like to take it in your room."

He looked around the table, and his gaze landed on me. Our eyes locked. "No thanks," he said. "I have places to be." He turned, walked off the deck, and settled into his beautiful car. Then, with a peal of tires on gravel, he was gone.

"The bloody cheek!" said a voice behind us. We turned quickly. Florian Craig stood by the coffee maker filling a mug. He plopped into a captain's chair across from me and Melody and poured a healthy dollop of cream into his coffee. For someone who'd been drinking scotch half the night he looked pretty good.

"Like I said, slick as a mole." Melody's mouth was set in a tight-lipped line. She raised her coffee mug in a toast and the four of us clinked. "He's staying here for the rest of the week," she said. "Unless he starts thinking he can boss me around. Then he's goin' back to Portland sooner." She seemed a bit crabby; maybe it was the murder. I certainly wasn't feeling any too good myself.

Angel rejoined us at the table with a plate of warm cinnamon rolls. She sat in the fourth chair. "I do not like that man," she muttered in heavily accented English. It sounded like a curse. "He is what my Zephyr calls 'bad news'."

At four-foot-ten, Angel not only was a great cook but a formidable observer of human nature. The last time she said she didn't like someone, he'd ended up dead. It had nothing to do with her.

"He was rude to Angel yesterday," said Melody. "One more strike and he's out."

"What do you mean he's going back to Portland?" I asked. "I thought he was from Nevada."

Melody shook her head. "*Was* being the operative word, sugar. Ol' Max lives in Portland now. That company he owns bought a building in the Pearl and is fixing it up for condos. He's up here managing things. I heard he got into some trouble down his way and needed to go somewhere for a while. Plus it gives him license to come to Oregon and do his shit-stirrin' up here."

I was all attention. Over the past ten years, Portland's Pearl District, once low-rent and industrial, had been gentrified off the charts after some far-sighted developers had converted old warehouses into trendy lofts and beautiful new condominium complexes. It now was home to up-market boutiques, galleries, and restaurants, not to mention people with yearly incomes higher than my net worth had been, and a smattering of real life celebrities.

Melody took a quick peek at her watch and stood. "Guess it's time to get ready to be hostess with the mostest. I better go make myself presentable."

Florian, who'd been immersed in his own thoughts for the past several minutes, looked at me across the table. "Are you going up to see Lila Ryder today, darling? If so, would you mind if I tagged along?"

"Not at all, Florian, I'd love that. I planned to drive up there after breakfast. Then Cat and I need to get back to Portland." We both needed to make certain everything in our gardens had plenty of water during this heat wave.

"I'm sorry you're going back, luv. If you stayed put a bit longer we could hunt murderers together."

I shot him a filthy look. I wasn't interested in hanging out with Florian if it involved looking for murderers. While he may have aptitude in that arena, I'd learned how much trouble an amateur like me could get into. I was having no part of it. "So you're staying for a while?" I asked.

"Of course I'm staying, darling. I'm not going to fly home until I've had a good look around. I'll be here for at least another week. I can file my columns from my laptop. Much better here than in The City in August."

I nodded my agreement. "All right then, let's eat and saddle up before it gets too hot."

The drive to the Ryder Estate included a trip down one hill, two miles of highway, and a winding three-mile climb up another hill.

Located in the Dundee Hills, the site had been hand-picked by James Ryder following exhaustive climatological studies. When the wine growing pioneers arrived in Oregon, most of them from California, the big questions looming for all of them was if *vitis vinifera*, the European grape stock from which the world's great wines are made, could be grown successfully in northwestern Oregon. Great pains were taken to find the warmest microclimates, and in the late 1960s the south-facing Dundee Hills were determined to be among the most suitable.

In the years before widespread drip irrigation, it took Ryder Estate and the smattering of other grape growing enthusiasts five years to get decent crops from their young vines, and several more years to set reasonable expectations for the wines. As the vineyards slowly matured, winemakers learned to work with the fruit and honed their skills. Nobody was getting big bank loans back then, or even small ones, for projects considered so risky. So everything moved forward gradually, over time, as the early vintners found alternate ways to purchase better equipment, good French oak barrels, and all the accoutrements it takes to produce world-class wines.

Even early on, despite the many challenges, there were the occasional, stupendously delicious wines—portents of what could be done with regularity once the vines matured, winemakers gained expertise, and more resources became available. These achievements were not lost on those of us who were paying attention.

As my car was without air-conditioning, we drove in Florian's rental car to the Ryder home. I rode shotgun and gave directions. "How long has it been since you've been to Oregon?" I asked him, as we bumped along a rising gravel county road.

Florian kept his eyes on the road. "Five years, darling," he said. "I was out here just once, briefly, and did all my wine tasting in a hotel in Portland. So this is new to me."

I remembered how he would laugh at me, during the years when I first met him at the East Coast wine competitions where I occasionally judged, about my unabashed enthusiasm for wines from the Northwest and their remarkable story. Now he was giving lectures on the glories of Northwest pinot noir. "About time you dragged your sorry ass out here," I said.

"It's really much more sophisticated than I would have thought," he said. The British wine trade, of course, think they invented wine.

I gave his shoulder a playful punch and gestured for him to turn into the next driveway. The long drive through vineyards to the Ryder Estate Winery and James and Lila's nearby home had been paved since my last visit. I tensed myself for seeing Lila again—not only because of James's death, but also because of her health situation. For a person with cancer, the huge shock of losing one's spouse must be particularly difficult. I thought of the many logistics involved for someone who'd so recently lost her primary support system, such as getting to medical appointments just for starters. I expected that she had a lot of friends. There also were three grown daughters, but except for Stephanie I didn't know where they had ended up.

We reached a Y in the driveway, and a sign directed guests to the right toward the winery. However, a sandwich board sign intended for these prospective visitors had been placed in front of the winery sign. "Sorry, closed today", it read. We took the road less traveled and drove about a hundred yards. A new house loomed before us in place of the century-old farmhouse that the Ryders had lived in for decades. Business had boomed for the Oregon wine industry since I'd left it, and those who had succeeded could finally afford some luxuries. The parking area in front of the beautiful, modern structure was crammed with vehicles, so we turned around, parked at the side of the drive, and walked back toward it.

The front door stood ajar. Florian pushed it open for me and we walked in through a lovely entry hall to a large open living room-dining room area. A tall, handsome woman with flaming red hair walked up to greet us. She wore a hot pink sleeveless blouse, cream-colored shantung silk trousers, and lots of expensive-looking jewelry. "Thank you for coming," she said. "I'm Regan Ryder."

I should have known. She reached out her hand and I took it. "Emma Golden," I said. "It's been a while."

Regan's face lit up like someone had just handed her another diamond. "Emma, how kind of you to come. How wonderful to see you!" Regan grabbed both of my hands and did the popular air kiss thing. "It's been so long!"

It had been about fifteen years ago, at Regan's wedding, when I'd last seen her. She was the oldest of the three Ryder daughters and had become, I'd heard, a successful trial attorney and the mother of two boys. "Let me introduce you to Florian Craig, who also knew your father," I said.

Regan turned all of her considerable attention on Florian. She grabbed his outstretched hand in both of hers and didn't miss a beat. "Oh, and you're with the *New York Times*, aren't you?" Big sparkly smile.

Florian put on his deepest and most formal voice. "Yes, darling, I am. And I'm so very sorry about your father. He was a wonderful man and will be sorely missed by all of us who knew him."

"Mom will be so pleased to see you." Regan positively gushed. I wasn't clear which of us she meant, and I didn't remember her as the gushing type. But *tempus fugit* and all that. I couldn't imagine

Lila being pleased about anything at this juncture. We kept moving as others were arriving behind us.

Florian looked at me and raised his eyebrows as we walked further into the large living space. Her behavior seemed a bit over the top, given her father's untimely death. But today I had promised myself to be at my best, which allowed no space for judgment. "Yeah," I said. "I've never seen her even remotely like this, but it's been a while. There's another one too, in addition to Stephanie."

People in the rooms were dwarfed by a ceiling that angled upward to huge windows and the light. The floor-to-ceiling windows overlooked south-facing vineyards, allowing Nature to play a major role in the overall ambiance. The rooms were filled with art—eclectic, fun, vibrant art. Bright modern paintings, whimsical sculptures, a couple of huge Asian jars in one corner. A custom-painted cabinet. It was a vast change from the old days of the humble farmhouse.

Lila sat by the windows in a sleek chair of dark crimson leather. She looked very small and wan, but her red hair was as thick, bright, and shiny as I remembered it. In fact, it was perfect. I quickly realized she was wearing a very good wig. She managed a small smile at us and nodded as we entered the room.

Other visitors stepped to the side. I walked up to Lila, bent down, and hugged her. "I'm so terribly, terribly sorry," I said. My words caught in my throat.

Behind me, Florian extended his hand and introduced himself. "My deepest condolences to you and your family, Mrs. Ryder," he said. "I was a great admirer of your husband."

Lila murmured a thank you. A woman I didn't recognize walked from the kitchen, which flowed beautifully into the dining and living rooms, and set a glass of iced tea on a little table next to Lila. She was medium height, plump. Her long, strawberry blonde hair boasted expensive highlights. Her pale green linen suit and four-inch heels screamed salesperson. "There are beverages on the counter, everyone, please help yourselves," she announced to the room in general. Then she zeroed in on us.

"This is my middle daughter, Morgan," said Lila, and introduced us both.

Morgan also brightened. "I remember you," she said to me. "Thanks for coming." She shook my hand and then Florian's, and they engaged in small talk pleasantries.

I turned my attention back to the recent widow. Since Lila had never been a close friend, I didn't feel that I knew her well. I'd always been much closer to James, but I wanted to support her in any way I could. "I know how much James cared for you," I said. She took my hand and held it in both of hers. "I'd just talked to him last night, and he was on his way home to see if you needed anything. So I just…I'm sorry."

A little tear leaked out of my left eye and started down my cheek. I quickly wiped it away. I hate it when people catch me crying. Lila looked me in the eye, and teared up as she patted my hand. "Thank you. I'm just so glad you're here. I know he thought the world of you."

I moved aside to let others pay their respects, and took in the details of the new home. I walked over to the wall of tall windows. Above me, I noticed, the roof protruded out several feet. Inside, insulating blinds pulled up from the bottoms of the windows. Out on the deck several people drank coffee or iced tea among clusters of large planters stuffed with lush, flowering summer annuals. Florian had moved out there and was talking to someone. Inside, I noticed, Stephanie slouched in a corner, her face a mask of gloom. I walked across the room, but by the time I'd gotten through a couple of clusters of people she'd moved on. I went in search of a cup of coffee, annoyed that I didn't know who Florian had been talking to, or anyone else here for that matter.

I've never been much of a mixer, unless I had a drink in my hand. I'd been up late and still felt horribly shaken by James's death. I filled a mug with coffee and searched for a place to land. In the living room I spotted a settee I hadn't noticed when entering the house. It was an amazing piece, long and low, featuring a single cushion about seven feet long, and gently curving, carved and upholstered armrests at each end. It looked like something from the 1920s and was upholstered in a flocked fabric in the William Morris style. Its pale green background set off the flocking, which was the same dark crimson color as Lila's chair. It was breathtaking.

I knew I needed to touch it. I walked toward it. No one was sitting on it, perhaps because it was so beautiful, but this is where I wanted to park my butt. I smoothed my hand over the shockingly colored flocked foliage before taking a seat. I thought of Gertrude Stein in Paris, the Lost Generation, salons. This was a salon-worthy, story-worthy settee.

A fabric tab tickled the back of my leg as I sat. I stood up, set my coffee on the low table to the side of it, and lifted the tab—not a lot, but just enough to see that the seat cushion lifted open to reveal a full-length storage area beneath it that held a couple of throws, pillows and a small stack of magazines.

I quickly closed the seat, and was just about to sit down again when I spotted my ex, Dwight, entering the room with Pamela Fontaine. He hadn't seen me, but she did and gave me what probably was her most pursed and disapproving look. I'd been caught in the act of snooping. The old cat! I gave her a dismissive gaze, then picked up my coffee and walked out onto the deck to join Florian and mingle.

People talked in urgent and hushed tones. As so often happens in tragedies, we clustered together trying to make sense of the thing that made no sense. For those of us who'd known James Ryder since the early days, the feelings of, "How could it have happened?" and "How can we go on?" were dominant. I, for one, couldn't imagine the wine industry without him. And yet no one of us is indispensable. Nor are we immortal. At his age James just as easily could have died of something else and the end result would be the same. He'd still be dead. Still, this felt so much worse. Murder is a violation, a taboo. Its evil had shaken the wine industry's inner sanctums. As I stood near Florian listening to the conversations, I realized all of us felt it.

Finally we left. It hadn't been that long, really. I had hoped to talk with Lila, sit down and have a real conversation. But in the aftermath of last night's tragedy it was impossible. She was barely holding herself together. She looked baffled by the many souls who crowded her home. And people kept arriving, bearing food, bottles of wine, and flowers. By the time we stepped out of the house more people were walking up the driveway and it promised to be a very long day for those inside. It was a relief to be outside. I could only imagine how overwhelmed Lila must be feeling.

Florian held the door open as I seated myself in his rental car. Then he got in and started the engine. "You were quiet in there, darling."

"I said what I needed to say to Lila," I said. "I'm still pretty overwhelmed by it all. What's she going to do now?"

Florian took the practical view. "What any other person would do in her place, I imagine. Grieve and move on."

"It's not that easy when you now are the head of a business and have cancer," I said.

"Listen, Emma. I don't know her, but Lila didn't get where she is by being a delicate flower. She's been out here doing this for forty years. And from the look of the crowd in there, she'll have plenty of support."

"You're right," I countered. "But it's not like he died a natural death. The circumstances of his death make it extra hard, I think. And James is down in the county morgue for God knows how long. Who even knows when they'll release the body so he can be properly laid to rest?"

Florian looked both ways at the stop sign and we pulled out onto the county road and started down the hill. It was nearly noon. I could see shimmering waves of heat rising from the vineyards around us. Once it got this warm, the grape vines temporarily shut down. Fortunately, in our climate, it cools enough in the evenings that the plants can respirate and regroup during the night. This helps keep the acids high in the grapes and results in wines that are brighter and crisper than are their counterparts from warmer climates. Good acid levels are a huge factor in giving Willamette Valley wines their charm.

"I know you're concerned about Lila, Emma," Florian said. "Just try to remember, this is clearly out of your control. Life will go on. It always does. The important thing now is to find the killer."

I found myself paying particular attention to the green that surrounded us. "You're right," I said.

CHAPTER 5

Back at the Westerly, Florian retired to his room to prepare for the big Passport to Pinot afternoon tasting at the IPNC. In deference to Lila Ryder, he'd missed the IPNC Sunday brunch. But for his purposes, the tasting provided a more practical way to review a large number of wines and also to set up appointments for the remainder of his stay.

I found Cat in the swimming pool. She was otherwise packed and ready to leave, so I headed into the kitchen. Angel had prepared a sendoff lunch for us with some of her heavenly *sopitas*. Melody stood at the prep sink paring some radishes, waiting for me. "Who was up there?" she wanted to know the minute I walked into the kitchen.

At the refrigerator I poured myself a huge glass of cold water, then I flopped in a chair at the familiar round table. "Tons of people, Melody. But I can't give you specifics. It's only changed a hundred and eighty degrees since I lived out here."

She joined me at the table with a bowl full of radishes from Dan's kitchen garden. "Yes, but you were out here for six weeks last fall," she reminded me. "You saw everybody then."

"The people I talked to today were Lila and the daughters," I said. "But I'm sure everybody else was there too, or would be soon. I just didn't know who most of them were."

Angel brought a platter of the *sopitas* to the table and sat down just as Cat entered the kitchen. I managed to down three *sopitas* while Melody continued to give me the third-degree about what was going on up at the Ryder Estate. I did the best I could—there just wasn't that much for me to tell.

"How is Senora Ryder today," Angel asked. "I know of her from my Zephyr. She is a nice lady."

"I think she's in shock, Angel," I said, hoping what I told her would satisfy Melody's curiosity as well. "A lot of people were showing up, as you might imagine. It looks like it's going to be a long day for her."

"My cousin Lucila is working as her housekeeper now," Angel said. "The senora is in good hands."

I nodded, pleased to know that Lucila had found a more pleasant place of employment after she discovered last October that she'd been working for a whack-job murderer. Meanwhile, the heat was making me edgy, my tummy was full, and I was done. I just wanted to get home.

It was not to be, however. No sooner had the table been cleared and the dishwasher loaded than a large black sedan that screamed law enforcement pulled up near the deck and my old friends from the Yamhill County Sheriff's Department, lieutenants Jeffers and Haymore, emerged. Melody admitted them to the kitchen.

They both flashed their badges so everyone knew who they were. "We'd like to have a word with Ms. Golden," said Jeffers. He enjoyed playing Bad Cop.

"Well, hello to you, too," I said, faking cheeriness. Melody, Cat, and Angel, with Winston in tow, scurried from the kitchen. "How about some iced tea?" They both nodded their affirmatives and I collected glasses, ice, tea, lemon, and sugar. We sat down at the round oak table.

I really shouldn't be so pissy about these guys. They actually saved my life several months back—after I found their killer for them. Still, I felt defensive around them. They didn't *like* me. They thought I interfered. At least that's what the shit fairies in my head told me every time I thought of the two of them. And every time, I had to reel myself in and ignore those little demons. The shit fairies are not my friends, and their persistent yakking gets me into crazy thinking all the time. I had to remind myself that these men didn't necessarily dislike me. They were normal people just doing their jobs. And I happened to be one of the vehicles toward that end. I could behave like an adult. I also knew I had nothing new to tell them.

We looked each other up and down. "Well, fellas. Knock yourselves out," I said.

Jeffers stirred some sugar into his tea and took a sip. "We need you to tell us again, in your own words, what happened last night," said Jeffers.

Here we go again. Still, I knew it was important. I started from the beginning all over again. I tried to remember everything in minute detail—the sounds and smells of the evening as I made my way from the Oak Grove toward my car, my thoughts at the time, the Honey Buckets as I neared them, the man who approached from my distant right as I reached out and pulled open the door, and the horrible feeling of being attacked.

"Did you see anyone leaving the scene as you approached?" Haymore asked. "Did you feel that someone may have been there waiting, watching? Or anyone moving away quickly?"

"No to both," I said. "My intuition is pretty good, but this came out of nowhere. I was paying attention to my surroundings, but believe me, I wasn't even thinking about trouble of this magnitude."

"I understand," said Jeffers. "The stabbing happened just a couple of minutes before you arrived. When you tried to open that door, Ryder hadn't even bled out, and the murder weapon had hit his aorta. Somebody got out of there really fast. He or she would have been covered with blood."

That certainly wasn't a reassuring thought. But alas, I'd seen nothing or nobody of interest. My mind turned to Max Weatherman—Mr. Cool the during the previous night's altercation, Mr. Cool again this morning. "What about Max Weatherman?" I said. "He was heading in the direction of the porta-potties after the fight. Have you talked to him?"

"Not as of this time," Haymore said. "He's on our list."

The questioning continued for another half hour. Questions and more questions. Different ways of asking the same questions. And then the handing off of cards in case I remembered something else.

"Do you have any suspects?" I queried.

The men stood from the table. Both of them eyed me sharply. "You know better than to ask a question like that," said Haymore. "If we did, I wouldn't tell you."

Of course I knew that, but it never hurts to ask.

"Let's just say there are persons of interest." Jeffers made little quote marks with his fingers.

The moment their car pulled away from the house, everyone thronged back into the room. Winston barked and ran around in circles sniffing the floor and corners for evidence of interlopers. Melody dived straight into the action. "What did they want" she demanded.

"Nothing exciting happened," I assured her. "They just wanted to ask me the same old questions they asked last night. I did not, and do not, have any more information. Now I want to go home."

I'm hot, tired, and upset, I wanted to add. But I didn't. Cat and I grabbed out overnight bags and loaded them into the car. After hugs all around, we finally wound our way down the long, flower-lined drive and hooked up with Highway 99W headed north. It was blistering hot in the car, and traffic headed back toward Portland from the coast was formidable. We stopped at Burgerville in Newberg for fresh raspberry smoothies, all in the interests of keeping our strength up. Then, as usually happens, caloric intake stimulated conversation.

"Who do you think did it?" said Cat, refreshed from our little break. The icy smoothie seemed to have awakened her from a near-comatose state.

"I have no idea who could or would have done it," I said. "I still can't believe James is dead. He's the first of the Old Guard to go—except for Caroline, of course. And she was sick." So much had happened the previous fall. In addition to everything else, my old and dear friend Caroline, another of the pioneering set, had died at Thanksgiving. "I can't imagine anyone I know out here doing such a thing. But the community has changed. There are a lot more people in the industry now—people who know him and could, for some reason, have issues with him."

"What about his family?"

That jolted me. "*His* family? Whatever made you say that?"

"I don't know. In the cop shows, don't they always suspect a family member first? And, aren't most victims known to their murderers? I mean, don't you ever watch *Dateline*? It's usually the husband, except in this case James *was* the husband."

As a matter of fact, I'd never even heard of *Dateline*. But I did know about the statistics regarding murderers and their victims and their acquaintance with each other. The fact is, James Ryder probably was acquainted in some way with more than half of the people at the Salmon Bake last night. And, as contentious as he could be at times, a handful of them most likely didn't care for him.

All of us who'd been involved in starting the wine industry had endured hardship. A lot of marriages had been troubled, though not—with the one notable exception I knew of—enough to kill each other. James, for all his good qualities, had been an absentee husband and father. There had been years of financial hardship. I knew the story well. There were times when I'd heard Lila Ryder complain to other women friends about James's lack of interest in her and the family—usually after she'd had a few glasses of wine. As my situation had been fairly similar, I had even joined in. A couple of times she had suspected James was being unfaithful, but I don't know if anything ever came of it. And then I thought of her that morning—shrunken, haunted, and fearful. "I don't think so," I said. "For one thing, Lila isn't physically capable."

Cat sighed. "Yes, but there are daughters, right?"

"Yeah, three of them, but—"

"Well, what about *them*?"

"Don't be ridiculous." But it wasn't a ridiculous question. "I don't know," I added. "I haven't seen or heard anything about them for years. Except for Stephanie last night, and then today, when I saw them all. Longshot. There would have to be a strong motive or it doesn't fly. Those girls have every opportunity given to them."

Cat shrugged and fanned herself with her hand. "Okay, a longshot. Who else?"

"Wow, I don't know. There were only about a thousand people milling around out there last night. You saw 'em. James knew people from all over the world, most benign, others probably not so much. But just suppose somebody outside the gathering wanted to kill him. Not likely, but at that time of night, dusk, anyone could slip onto the campus unnoticed and do it."

"And then," said Cat, "there is always Max Weatherman."

"He's probably the logical choice, given their very public brawl," I said. "I don't know, though. Truth be told, he seems like a bit of a fop to me."

Cat snorted. "Such a lovely, out-of-date word, that."

"Yes, but look at him," I countered. "The fake tan, the sockless shoes. Even if he was going to kill someone, it wouldn't be bloody. He even wears a necklace."

"Don't knock 'em, just because you're into cowboys," said Cat. "Florian wears a gold chain too."

Aha, Cat had brought up Florian. "Florian's not a fop," I said. "And he could drop Max Weatherman on his four-hundred-dollar haircut faster than I can blink."

"Ooh, a bad boy." And then Cat took another turn. "What if he wasn't the intended victim?" That gave us something to think about in slow traffic with no air conditioning.

"You mean like some pissed-off woman came after her husband and got the wrong guy?" I said. "I was out there, it was nearly dark. Somebody could have pulled open the wrong door I suppose." I would mull that one, of course, but not very seriously.

"It's another long shot," said Cat. "Everybody has enemies, I suppose."

We didn't talk much during the rest of the drive. In fact, we both were nearly brain-dead from the heat. I dropped Cat at her house, and finally arrived at my own. Not only was it stinking hot inside, but also lonely. I watered the outside plants, which showed signs of heat stress. Then I went inside, filled the bathtub with tepid water, and submerged myself to cool off.

By seven, the temperature had started to drop a bit. I opened all the windows and turned up the fan and positioned it to draw the cooling air inside. I scrounged something from the refrigerator for dinner and took it outside where I plopped in my favorite director chair and ate. It was too warm to stay inside, and I was far too restless to sit. I washed my few dishes, donned walking shoes, and filled my water bottle.

It was a quiet evening in the neighborhood. This is the time of year when Portlanders vacation. It's hot in the city, and they can depend on the weather being good wherever they're going. I locked my front door and began walking through the neighborhood, winding my way uphill via deserted side streets, watching lights coming on in the houses as I passed them, until I reached the top of Council Crest. To the east, the city sprawled before me. A cooling breeze riffled my hair and cooled my face.

Physically drained I took a long drink from my water bottle. I sat on the bench adjacent the landmark Sacajawea statue. While I appeared to be at peace, I struggled with tangled and disturbed thoughts. Last night's violence had awakened the beast that had been sleeping in me since that disastrous trip to Bandon in early March. It had been an innocent enough road trip with Melody to find her sister, who had shacked up with an awful man. It ended in the death of someone very dear to me. For months I had been wrangling with the knowledge that I was, if one connected all the horrible dots, responsible for his death.

I had stuck my nose into a situation I should have avoided. Even with the extenuating circumstances, at one decisive moment I had made the decision that pushed things forward to their exploding point. At the time I'd been able to justify that decision. I was helping someone. I believed I needed to protect someone. But in the end, as often happens, that decision, made without looking at all the potential consequences, didn't wash. I would live with the consequences of those actions for the rest of my life.

For some time I had been too much in shock to fully comprehend my role. Today was different. Today James was dead, and someone was responsible. Bringing that person to justice was someone else's job. I had to carry that thought with me, to remind myself that no matter what, this crime was none of my business.

All around me people enjoyed the warm summer night. They walked their dogs, threw Frisbees, or sat on blankets spread on the vast surrounding lawn. Their voices rose and fell on the light evening breeze. On the road encircling the statue, cars filled with young lovers parked. Couples got out and walked around the statue holding hands, then flopped on the grass for a while before returning to their vehicles. A police car prowled lazily around the circle and, seeing nothing amiss, departed.

People came. People went. I sat, letting my thoughts solidify. Watching the city lights that sprawled and twinkled below me until the park closed, I processed my uncomfortable truth and let it become a part of who I am. It had been errant behavior with tragic consequences. I didn't know how or if I ever would forgive myself for what had happened. But my ability to influence that horrible outcome was long past. Somehow I would have to live with it.

It was late, and time for the park to close. Folks on the lawn stood, stretched, and slowly gathered their blankets and snacks. Car engines started, and we quietly took our leave. I walked home carefully, watching my step to avoid tripping on a curb or loose rock, smelling the flowers, alert but not concerned. I hadn't solved the murder, but my mind was clear. I was willing to accept James's death and what he had meant in my life. I could do that.

CHAPTER 6

Dawn's rosy fingers crept over the eastern horizon. I'd gone to bed after midnight and had slept badly. Even when I was able to sleep, I had suffered horrible dreams in which I repeatedly tried to remove bloody, sticky clothing from my body. In my dreams, the smell of warm blood made me gag. I'd jerk awake, terrified, only to doze off into another bloody milieu.

I stumbled into the kitchen and set about making coffee. I hadn't written in my notebook the previous night because I was too tired, but I had walked and thought about things a lot. The takeaway was this: I was not involved. Yes, it all had been horrible, but unless the authorities needed to talk to me yet again, I was out of the picture. I'd return to wine country for James's memorial, and that would be the end of the story.

Since I was no longer a part of the community, there was no need to do more. I hadn't socialized with anyone involved in the Yamhill County wine scene since I'd moved to Portland. I had touched base with a number of players to update research for my upcoming book, but otherwise I was done with that life. It had taken me eight years, but over the past several months I had been able to let that part of my history go with acceptance. Thank God.

With that, I busied myself for the rest of the day, catching up on chores in the yard, changing the sheets on my bed, and doing a complete housecleaning. Tuesday followed the same pattern of organizing and catching up. Late afternoon, after shopping for groceries, I flopped on the sofa with a book and relaxed. The heat was less intense, and it now was possible to rest comfortably in my home. While busy, my mind stayed in a good place. At rest, it seemed to go wild. The shock and sadness of James's death kept bubbling up. Yes, I told myself again and again, he was gone. Justice would be done and there was nothing I could do.

I dozed off briefly, only to be awakened by the chirrup of my cell phone. I looked at the screen. Melody. "Well, hello to you too," I said into the phone.

"Oh hi, Emma," she said. "I just wanted to let you to know that James's memorial will be Saturday afternoon on the Linfield campus."

I quickly digested the information. "Thanks, Mel. Where, specifically."

"The Oak Grove. I guess the auditorium there is too small."

The auditorium was way too small. Tons of people would want to attend James's final send-off.

"Yes," she continued, "I heard that all the restaurants are getting together to provide refreshments. It's going to be quite the do. Bagpipes and the works."

"Yes, it sound like it's going to be a big deal," I said. "What else do you know?"

"Well…." Melody paused and took a deep breath. "Guess who didn't come home last night?"

She'd hooked me. Again. "Uhhh…." I wracked my brain. Florian. He'd caught up with Cat—who at times could be more closed-mouth than anyone I knew. I hadn't heard from her since Sunday. Perhaps he'd taken her out, wooed the heck out of her, then spent the night at her place, and she'd never even bothered to call me. "Florian Craig!" I was sure of it.

"Nope. Guess again."

"Melody, enough. I don't have time for this."

"You're no fun." There was a short, dramatic pause so the truth of the statement would sink in. "But, no. Florian's here. He just parked his ample rear on the front porch with a glass of iced tea. He spent the day out shakin' the bushes in the name of journalistic excellence."

"So, who didn't come home that has you so upset?"

"Who says I'm upset?"

"Melody!" I said. "Enough!"

"Max Weatherman. He's not out there. Took off yesterday mid-afternoon and hasn't been back."

Being an innkeeper, Melody pays attention in detail to the comings and goings of all her guests. That's one reason she's so good at keeping them happy. "So, it's got your attention," I said. "But how big of a deal is this really? Maybe he hooked up with that leggy woman he was chasing on Saturday night. And why do you care?"

Melody thought about it, but not for long. "I probably don't," she said. "I do miss looking at his car. He's paid up through the week, so that's not a concern. But your deputy friends were here today wanting to chat with him. So maybe he's a suspect."

"Maybe. But you and I both know they're talking to everyone, suspect or not. I wouldn't put much stock in that."

"You're right." She sounded a little miffed that I hadn't jumped into her drama with her. "He's just off chasin' women like the old tom cat he thinks he is." She chortled to herself. "But hey, I've got your suite here ready for you on Saturday if you want to spend the night after the memorial."

"Oh, I'd love that. Thanks." I doubtless would need someone to talk to after the ordeal. And Melody always saw things a little differently than I. So we could relax and snack and just be girlfriends and process everything that happened that day. "I'll stop by early Saturday and we can go together."

"You got it." She hung up.

I roused myself from the elusive nap. Melody had gotten my brain running again, and further rest was out of the question. So our friend Max Weatherman had gone AWOL. Hmmm. A person isn't necessarily involved in something if she just wants to satisfy her curiosity, I told myself as I booted up my laptop and did a little search. He lived somewhere in Portland, I knew from information I'd picked up during the weekend. His company built condominiums, or so I'd been led to believe. I Googled Max Weatherman, and yes, there he was. Henderson, Nevada. WeatherVane Enterprises. The site even showed a picture of him looking all tan and slicked back and oily in an expensive Italian summer suit. That was much easier than I thought it would be.

After a complete perusal of the WeatherVane website, I returned to the "Properties" tab and slowly made my way through the company's list of projects. And there it was, near the top of the list—WeatherVane West, with 122 deluxe condominiums offered for pre-sale at its new South Waterfront location. One-bedroom units started at $345,000—more if you wanted a view of the Willamette River. Lucky purchasers could choose their own colors and finishes. Such a deal.

In addition to joining the building boom at Portland's South Waterfront, the company had purchased an extant condominium complex in Portland's upscale Pearl District and were in the process of renovating the vacant units. Since he didn't look like the camping type, this presumably is where Max Weatherman was holed up when he wasn't making trouble in wine country.

With nothing better to do, I hopped a downtown bus to the Pearl District to have a look around. I hadn't been to the area for several months. Building activity was rampant with sidewalk detours, scaffolds running up buildings, and traffic blocked on several streets. Business people and shoppers moved with purpose in the late-afternoon heat. I walked the district, noticing new restaurants and wandering into interesting-looking shops. I passed the WeatherVane-owned complex. It featured a 24-hour doorman—a bit high-flying for Portland, but it did give me someone to chat up. I learned about the private gym, and other amenities important to people with a lot more money than me. However, when I mentioned my old buddy Max Weatherman, the nice doorman was completely closed-mouth.

It occurred to me that I probably wasn't going to see Weatherman window-shopping in the neighborhood, but one never knows. I'd spotted Gus Van Sant down there the previous summer. I pictured myself bumping into Weatherman on the street. "Oh, hi

Max," I'd say. "What a coincidence." In my fantasy, we'd go have a coffee. That is, if he didn't run across the street to avoid having eye contact with a woman of my age. It happened.

An hour later I was on the bus headed home. I really was nosy, and there was no excuse for it. Why did I care anyway? I didn't have time to waste sticking my nose where it didn't belong.

My cell phone chirped as I entered my home. Melody again. She was breathless. "You'll never believe what happened," she began.

She was right—I wouldn't. But before I could even respond, she started talking again. "Two creepy looking men came here this afternoon looking for Max Weatherman. They drove a big, black Humvee with tinted windows and Nevada license plates, and they had an attitude. They wanted to find old Max, and they wanted to find him right *now*."

My mind took the huge leap into race mode. "Okay? What did you tell them?"

Melody—what a piece of work. Through cyberspace I could almost feel her puffing herself up like a hen. "Well, I told them I didn't *know* where he is. They wanted to see his room, and I said 'No *sir*, it's rented to him. You can't see it, not unless you're law enforcement and have a warrant.'"

I thought briefly about my experience with the FBI, and how it moves in mysterious ways, its wonders to behold. "And do you think they might *be* law enforcement?"

"No *ma'am*, they aren't law enforcement." She was indignant that I'd even suggest such a thing. "These guys were thugs! I could just tell. They both wore sunglasses and had gold chains around their necks. How many FBI agents do you know who don't identify themselves, and who wear big gold chains? And drive Humvees? These two were *mafia dons*! I just know it!"

By now Melody was in high dudgeon. She's really good at high dudgeon. "Where's Florian?" I asked. I was willing to bet money these guys were not mafia dons, and that Florian Craig would know exactly how to handle a pair of thugs.

"Oh, I don't know where he went. He was here a while ago, but he's out again messing around visiting wineries and yakkin' with people. And later tonight he'll be off seeing your friend. You know. I don't see much of him. But I didn't like these guys. Not one bit. They were pushy and rude, and one of them looked like a weasel."

Great. "Well, you might want to have a little nightcap with Florian when he gets in tonight, just so he's up to speed," I said. I didn't mention that Melody might also want to sleep with what she calls her "baby Glock" under her pillow. If I knew Melody, she'd figure that out by herself.

"What good can Florian do?" she wondered.

Oh, you'd be surprised, I thought. I had not told Melody that I suspected my former wine circles colleague had a past life, perhaps as a special operative for the British government. I had no solid evidence of such a career, but Florian always managed to be vague about the many years of his professional life between college graduation and prior to the wine writing. He'd spent much of it in northern Africa and the Middle East, which is not where most young men brought up in the British wine trade are wont to spend much time. I never could get any more information from him on the subject, and God knows I'd tried! Since that was all I knew, my imagination had supplied the rest. I merely said, "He's a beefy boy. I imagine if those guys come back he could send them on their way more convincingly than you."

Melody grabbed the thought enthusiastically. "Great idea, thanks," she said. "I'll wait up for him."

As soon as we rang off, I realized I had a roaring appetite. I picked some frisee from the kitchen garden, poached two eggs, and made myself a delicious salad for dinner. Then, following a brief walk around the neighborhood, I settled in to watch a couple episodes of "Midsomer Murders" on DVD.

At two in the morning the heat wave of the past week finally broke. I was awakened by huge claps of thunder. Lightning flashed my bedroom bright white, then black, then white again. Across the back yard I watched the trees, limbs bouncing, bent by heavy wind gusts. The heavens opened to a glorious, cleansing rain that cleared the air and soaked the parched earth. I stood at my bedroom window watching the storm, feeling the temperature drop to a comfortable level. And then the rain stopped as abruptly as it began, and I returned to bed, and to sleep.

Troubled sleep dogged me the remainder of the night. I awoke again and again, restless and sticky with sweat. As the sky began to lighten I finally slept hard and dreamed hard. In my dream, James Ryder stumbled toward me along a rocky path. The blood on his clothing had crusted down the front of him. His bloodied white hair streamed across his face. Eyes wild, he reached to me, but he didn't so much see me as look through me. He cried out, "No, not you. Anyone but you!" I jerked awake, terrified and confused. It was broad daylight.

CHAPTER 7

Saturday morning. An amazingly beautiful summer day. The day of James Ryder's memorial. I hadn't talked to Melody since our conversation about the "thugs". My mind flicked over the few details I remembered from what she'd told me earlier as I packed an overnight bag. If they'd come back, if there had been any drama whatsoever, she would have called. Not a peep. I assumed all was well.

My miserable wardrobe yielded a variety of the usual disappointments. I had blown my budget on the cute dress I'd worn to the Salmon Bake, only to have it ruined. It would have been a nice dress to wear to the memorial—nice, seasonal, not too flashy. Yes. It would have been perfect. I dug around in the closet, growing grumpier as I failed to turn up anything I deemed suitable. At last I settled on a skirt nobody, including myself, had set eyes on for at least six years, a white tank top, and a colorful summery scarf. Simple and comfortable. Invisible. It would have to do.

I pulled up at the Westerly at noon, grabbed my bag from the trunk, and walked up onto the back porch. Before moseying into the kitchen, I had a good look around at gardeners gardening, a couple playing tennis, a family enjoying the swimming pool, all the very picture of peace and serenity. I walked through the sliding glass door and set down my bag. Angel stood at the cooktop. Luscious smells emanated from a large sauté pan.

"Hey Angel!" I set my bag on the floor. Winston tore into the kitchen to greet me, yapping crazily.

Angel turned toward me and flashed her huge grin. "Oh Senora, you are just in time. I am making your favorite lunch."

I walked over and hugged her, sneaking a peek over the top of her head to see what she was stirring. A thick red chili tomato sauce by the look of it. I wasn't sure what my favorite lunch was, but anything Angel cooked was fine by me.

Melody swept into the room and grabbed me by the arms. Air kiss, air kiss. "I'm so glad you're here," she said.

I drew back. "Where are the thugs?"

Melody produced an easy laugh. "I think I scared them off," she said. "They haven't been back. Neither has Max Weatherman. I don't know where he went, but he's not here. Probably went back to Portland where he belongs. We packed up his stuff yesterday morning, and it's in the basement waiting for himself to come back and collect it. Some new guests, a family, checked into the Carriage House yesterday."

Interestinger and interestinger. "A puzzle for sure," I said. "What do you think happened to him?"

"I don't know and I don't care," said Melody. She flounced over to the refrigerator, opened it, and removed a pitcher of iced tea. "He got distracted. Maybe he knew those guys were coming after him and went back to Nevada. We'll find out, I guess, when he comes to retrieve his clothes. I *do* plan to ask."

Well, of course she did. I headed for the table a couple steps behind Angel. My favorite lunch was being served. "If you're happy, I'm happy," I said. "Not my problem."

Melody poured tea all around and seated herself. "That's right. Now," she pointed a finger in my direction, "don't you eat too much. I know it's good, but we're going to have a whole lot of food at the memorial."

"Yes, ma'am," I said, and we dug in.

Half an hour later, I wandered up the narrow stairway to my private lair and placed my bag on the luggage rack. I turned to flop onto the bed, and there, to my great surprise, was the sundress. I picked it up and examined it. Was it mine or was it a replacement? How? Or why? The fabric was crisp, the bloodstains were gone. Not a sign of them. It had to be new. Nothing short of an act of God could have gotten all that blood out. I didn't think God had time to worry about such a thing as a ruined frock, so Melody must have intervened. I removed the skirt and top I was wearing and carefully tried it on. I turned around in front of the mirror.

Someone knocked on the stairway door below. The door opened and Winston bounded up the stairs and into my room, followed by Melody. "Hey, look at you," she said. She walked up behind me and looked in the mirror. "Angel told me she could salvage it, but I didn't believe her."

"You're lying through your teeth," I said. Melody just smiled her most inscrutable smile. The two of us looked at our reflection in the mirror. With heels on, she was only a couple inches shorter than I. She reached up and draped something over my shoulders. "This way you won't get cold in the shade." She adjusted the chiffon-y little wrap she'd purloined from her own wardrobe, then stood back and admired the effect.

It dressed me up and covered my upper arms. "Perfect," I said. "And thank you. This is a very special gift." For a short moment I felt like we were sisters, joined at the hip by the Universe for some mysterious purpose we'd never understand.

Melody put her hands on my shoulders and gave a little squeeze. "We need to leave in ten minutes," she said. "See you downstairs."

I stood there for another couple moments reflecting on our long on-and-off history. The one thing I knew for sure about Melody, besides the fact that she's a character, is that she is the real deal, a true friend. We both could get our undies in a wad sometimes about who did what to whom, whose fault it was, what have you. But I knew that she had my back and I had hers. I was pretty certain it would stay that way as long as we both drew breath.

We arrived at the Oak Grove at two-thirty. By the time we'd parked Melody's Mini Cooper and made it onto the Linfield campus, most of the hundreds of the folding chairs were taken and people had gathered in standing groups under several of the large oak trees. We managed to find a couple of chairs near the back of the seating area. A stage had been set up at the front, complete with a podium flanked by two huge sprays of summer flowers. Another several dozen floral arrangements crowded the space in front of the stage. A large screen rose behind it.

The minute we sat, we began craning our necks to see who was there. Melody pointed out a number of people I knew from the past but otherwise wouldn't have recognized, plus some of the more notable newcomers. I stood up to have a better look around, and Lo! My two favorite detectives lurked in the shade of an oak tree. They wore blue blazers and khaki slacks. With their stern looks and with sunglasses concealing distinguishing features, they looked ridiculously like "Men in Black". In front of them stood two somewhat shorter men also wearing sunglasses. Their bright Hawaiian shirts set them apart from less casually dressed attendees. One of them looked like a weasel.

I sat down and nudged Melody with my elbow. "Look over there." My head jerked in the direction of the detectives. "Recognize anyone?"

Melody looked, and then put her hand to her mouth. "Jesus, Mary, and all the saints!" she said. "It's the thugs. I wonder what *they're* doing here."

No sooner were the words out of her mouth when the weasel spotted us and nudged his sidekick. I could feel the two sets of eyes on us even though I couldn't see them.

"Shit," said Melody.

"Yes. At a memorial for someone they probably never met," I said.

"The cheek, as Florian would say," Melody said. "I wonder if they're still looking for their friend Max Weatherman."

At that moment, Florian Craig appeared, bumbling in front of seated mourners, making his way clumsily toward us. He wore a stylish blazer, open neck dress shirt, and crisp pressed slacks. He dropped abruptly in the empty seat next to Melody and jutted his head out so he could make eye contact with both of us. "Good afternoon, ladies. Mind if I sit here?"

"Not at all," said Melody.

"Make yourself comfortable," I said.

"And, oh, by the way." Melody gestured over her shoulder toward the thugs. "Those are the creeps that came by the house looking for Max Weatherman the other day. As you know, I've been sleeping with my gun ever since."

Florian, who had heard all about them, probably more than once, turned his glance toward the tree sheltering Haymore, Jeffers, and the thugs. "Really, darling," he said after taking them in for a moment. "I think I'll go and have a dickey with those blokes. If you'll just excuse me, ladies."

"Of course," said Melody.

"Take all the time you need," I chimed in.

Florian lumbered to his feet and maneuvered his large body back the way he'd come. It was slow going, and he was treated to several foul glances and grumpy asides. Once free of the constricting row of seats, he rearranged himself and strode confidently in the direction of his unsuspecting victims. As I watched, a little thrill raced through me.

He walked up to the two strangers, smiling and nodding pleasantly. They shook hands all around and spoke for a minute. The detectives behind them began watching with growing interest. With a gesture, Florian led the men from under the tree and away from the detectives. Then his entire demeanor changed. His brow furrowed and the friendliness left his face. He spoke rapidly and even touched an index finger to the weasel's chest. The weasel and his pal backed up a step. Their faces slackened. Florian then gave a curt nod, turned away from them, and made his way back to the chairs and once again in front of the grouches.

He took his seat next to Melody and gave her a big smile. His broad face had gone red, but otherwise he looked pleasant and bland. "I don't think they'll be bothering you again, darling," he said.

"What did you say?" I blurted.

Florian smiled benignly in my direction. "Not to worry, darling," was all he said. Rats! I looked over my shoulder to where the thugs had stood. Haymore looked at his watch. Jeffers yawned and scanned the crowd. The other two men were nowhere in sight.

Lila arrived in a wheelchair pushed by a very cute young man I later learned was her 13-year-old grandson, firstborn of daughter Regan. Regan, the eldest of the Ryders' three children, followed her wearing a stylish beige suit with a short skirt and four-inch heels, red hair flashing in the sun. She held the hand of a little boy, who couldn't stop jumping and also sported flaming red hair that reminded me of Lila in her younger days. Regan's distinguished-looking husband—silver fox in expensive suit—brought up the rear.

I observed Regan's expression—somewhat stern but cool, in charge. She was hands-down the best dressed woman at the event.

Melody, following my gaze, leaned toward me and said, "She made full partner at her law firm last year. They *gave* her a membership at the Multnomah Athletic Club."

"Must be nice," I murmured. A membership at MAC cost more than my net worth.

Daughter Number Two, Morgan, filed in behind Regan's family. Second child, she was the keeper of two youngsters, twins apparently, a boy and a girl who looked about eight or nine. As with Regan, Morgan had changed so much in the dozen or so years since I'd seen her that I wouldn't have recognized her if I hadn't seen her the previous Sunday at Lila's house. She gripped the children's hands as she steered them toward their seats—a curly strawberry blond with two adorable little strawberry blonds in sailors' outfits. Morgan was no longer the cute, carefree girl I'd known. She'd gotten quite fat. But it was her expression that was more noticeable than the weight gain. It was worried and anxious, haunted.

"Nasty divorce last year," Melody said in stage whisper. I nodded. Morgan had always been the cute one. Pink dresses. Homecoming queen. I didn't know what she was up to now. As if reading my mind, Melody added, "Elementary school teacher, Beaverton Public Schools."

And then there was Stephanie, the youngest. I had not talked to her up at the Ryder home the previous Sunday. Blond greasy hair fell across her shoulders. Once again, she wore inappropriate clothes that were too small for her. The overall effect was not good. "Oh dear," I said before I could stop myself.

"What on earth was she thinking?" said Melody.

She, more than anyone I'd seen that day, appeared to be in genuine pain. She was unkempt, which could signal grieving. Or, maybe it was an aspect of depression. Or, maybe she just didn't give a rip. When she was young, I remembered a shy, quiet girl, always hanging behind her father, holding onto his hand, while the two older girls strutted their stuff. She'd taken up the mantle for the winery and made her parents proud. But one did wonder what was going on with her that she wouldn't or couldn't take care of herself.

The memorial itself ran an hour and a half, a well-orchestrated production designed to maximize James Ryder's many accomplishments. There were no family testimonials, none of the usual homespun stuff. This was a big deal. Many dignitaries including Oregon's governor thanked James posthumously for his contributions to a now nearly two-billion-dollar industry. The result made for a somewhat sanitized version of James's amazing life, but the slideshow captured him perfectly—the infectious smile, the awards, the larger than life man who bit off a huge chunk and against the odds found himself able to chew it. I was moved to tears just remembering him in some of those situations. That he had come to such a horrible end seemed of relatively small import compared to the huge contributions he'd made in life. He had accomplished what he set out to do. How many of us, I wondered, actually manage to do that?

Relieved when the ordeal finally was over, I stood. My legs nearly buckled beneath me. Florian, who was paying more attention than Melody, grabbed me by the arm. "Take a deep breath, darling," he said. "It's too bad you no longer imbibe. You could do with one." He pulled a silver flask from his jacket pocket, unscrewed the cap, and passed it to Melody. She smiled her wicked smile, took a swig, and handed it back to him, whereupon he took and equally generous swig, recapped the flask, and returned it to his pocket.

Food trays began circulating from several small tents surrounding the Oak Grove. We moved toward them. I needed food quickly to dispel my wooziness, and we were treated to the best Yamhill County restaurants had to offer. We went our separate ways, my friends to check out the wines and I to cut as wide a swath as possible through the abundant selection of delicious refreshments.

Unfortunately, the food idyll lasted a shorter duration than I would have wished. I managed to nosh down several of the more interesting items circulating, but as usual, the anticipation of the food far exceeded my ability to consume it. I was quickly sated and in danger of becoming bored when I espied my ex and Pamela lurking near a tray of particularly enticing hors d'oeuvre. Turning quickly to avoid having to talk to them, I bumped into Rob Grimes, police reporter for the local bi-weekly newspaper.

Rob juggled a small plate piled high with food and a glass of red wine. "Emma, great to see you!" He looked surprised as he flubbed around trying to free a hand so we could shake.

I signaled for him to relax. "Hi Rob. Don't bother. Great to see you, too. What are you doing here?" Rob was a long way from his normal beat—crime and education—and I knew he hadn't known James Ryder.

Rob popped a meaty morsel into his mouth and chewed for a moment. "You know, don't you, that since last fall they've added the wine industry to my beat?"

It made sense. Rob had learned a lot about the wine industry over the past several months. I am happy to say that I had directed him toward much of that knowledge. "So, are you here for the wine angle or the police angle?" I had to ask. One thing I'd quickly learned about Rob is that he wasn't stingy with his information.

He shrugged and took a sip of wine and looked around as if he was concerned about being overheard. "It could go either way," he said. "Mainly I'm here to cover the memorial. But since it was a murder with a very active investigation who knows what might turn up."

I looked around too, just in case. "Well, I did see Haymore and Jeffers here before things got started…."

"Yeah, they're here, along with some other people you probably wouldn't notice," Rob said. "I know they really want to talk to Max Weatherman and they haven't been able to locate him—either out here or at his place in Portland. They were hoping he'd show up here today."

I loved learning what those who serve and protect are up to. And, I was always happy to give Rob any information that might lead to a story or help him out. "He was staying at the Westerly," I told him. "But then he up and left. He'd paid through the week. If you see him, tell him he can stop by any time and get his stuff."

"The detectives think he's gone back to Henderson." Rob took another enormous bite of something.

"That's interesting but doubtful," I said. "Melody told me two creepy guys came to the Westerly a couple days ago. They were driving a black customized Humvee with Nevada plates. And I saw them here this afternoon right before the service started—or, rather, Melody did. If they'd located him, they wouldn't still be hanging around."

Rob was clearly interested. He quit eating. "Wow, that's great information. Do the guys know?"

"If they're paying attention," I said. "But I don't know. Not my circus, not my monkeys." I felt a little smug. I'd been working on my boundary issues for the past several months. Titillating as it all was to me, this was none of my business. "I just want the murderer to be caught. James was a personal friend."

"Well, I'm going to tell them."

"Knock yourself out. Just remember I don't know anything about it. If they need to talk to someone they can talk to Melody."

Rob eyed me suspiciously. "You're not interested?"

"I'm interested in the outcome. Period. I just want to see justice served. I've had enough excitement in the last year to last me a lifetime." I meant it.

"Well, gee," he said. "Thanks for the tip. I really appreciate it."

"Sure," I said. "And if you're interested in a feature, the wine columnist for *The New York Times* is in town. Florian Craig. He's another old friend. He's going to be in the area for the next week or so. He'd be a great interview, and he's also staying at the Westerly."

Rob grinned, obviously pleased. "Thanks again." The food had disappeared. He reached out and shook my hand.

"Pshaw," I said, shaking his hand. Then I gave him a big hug. "It was a real treat to see you, Rob. Give my best to Janine and the kids."

Rob turned away from me, probably in search of more food. I scanned the crowd for signs of Melody. My old pals Restless, Irritable, and Discontent were tuning up in that space between my ears, a combination of my discomfort in crowds and the nature of the occasion. In deference to them and the havoc they could wreak, I wanted to go home. I spotted Melody over by one of the white tents, glass of wine in hand, head thrown back in laughter. As I began my press to reach her, a cacophony of male voices erupted to my right. At first I thought it was a fight. God help us, not another one. But there was laughter, and then the voices burst into song.

Distracted, I turned in the direction of the singing. I recognized that fine baritone as belonging to my former husband. Several men, most of them old-timers, but a few new faces as well, stood in a circle. They sang Auld Lang Syne at the top of their lungs, and it was beautiful. Other people gathered around them and began singing along. The bag-pipers set down their wine glasses and began blowing their pipes.

One of our old friends, pioneer winemaker Michael Delaney, widower of my late friend Caroline, saw me standing at the edge of the group and pulled me toward the circle. "Come on, Emma," he yelled. "If anyone belongs here, you do!" And then there I was among them feeling, for the moment at least, as if I'd never left. As if I still belonged. I realized I'd probably be here for a while longer.

As my voice joined in with the others, my eyes panned the crowd. Across from me, a bottle of scotch was passed from man to man. Behind Dwight I could see Pamela, arms folded, lips pursed, looking for all the world as if she was in desperate need of a kale smoothie. Melody's face popped into the panorama. She spotted me and gave thumbs up. Florian shoved his way into the circle, grabbed the scotch bottle, took a swig, and joined in the singing.

The governor and other dignitaries had long since departed and we were left with who we were. The singing continued, but I left the circle, ever mindful of the scotch bottle and its progress toward me. This was not a time for me to be tempted. I scooted around the back of the circle to find Melody and grabbed her arm. Melody's color was up as she'd been singing too. "Just like the old times," she said.

How I wished, for probably the millionth time, it still was the old times—without my addiction, of course. I felt a lump in my throat. "Yeah, it is," I said. And those were all the words I could get out. I gave her arm a little squeeze and left the group. I needed to pay my respects to the Ryder family before we left, and it was past time for me to leave.

I easily located Lila near the edge of the Oak Gove. She sat at a small table talking with a couple I didn't know. Stephanie lurked a few yards from her; the other two daughters stood farther away near one of the restaurant tents. They were deep in conversation. As I neared the table, the couple stood and took their leave.

I gave Lila a gentle hug and sat down beside her. She looked beyond exhausted. "How's it going?" I asked her. "Can I get you anything?"

She smiled at me with her mouth but not her eyes. "Some water would be nice."

I trotted over to the nearest food tent where I located a bottle of sparkling water and a two plastic cups. I then returned to Lila and poured us each some of the water. "That was a wonderful memorial," I said. "You covered all the bases. James would be so pleased."

Lila took a couple sips of the water and looked in the direction of the singing. Then her eyes met mine and I saw the defeat in her expression. "Thank you," she said. "We did what was expected. I think it went very well. But the real memorial is just getting started." She gestured toward the singers. "Unfortunately, I'm not feeling well enough to participate."

We sat in the beautiful Oak Grove not speaking. As people took wandered toward their cars, they stopped by the table with condolences and offers to help out. I stayed quiet, unnoticed except for brief greetings to the ones I knew. Nearby, Stephanie had filled a plate of food and was eating, watching. It felt as if she was standing guard over her mother. Morgan and Regan had moved closer to the singers, but remained glued together, talking intently. I'd once again lost track of Melody, but it was good. I was mellow, just sitting with an old friend.

By now most of the mourners had left except for the group of twenty or so, mostly male, mostly the core group of James and Lila's oldest friends and founders of the wine industry. It struck me as a little odd that the daughters were not with their mother at the table. She wouldn't be here either, I reasoned, except by necessity. In normal times, she would have been over there in the middle of the group. Between the songs, people told stories punctuated with loud laughter.

"How are you holding up?" I asked Lila.

She looked at me briefly. "In what way?"

"In any way. Emotionally. You're ill. Are you going to have enough support? What are you going to do now that the memorial is over? From my experience, this is when it gets tough."

Lila sighed, took another sip of water. "I don't know," she said. "What I'm going to do, I mean. I'm a wreck. You know what it's like. I'm in shock. I miss my best friend. It's awful. Stephanie isn't emotionally available, or present. For the type of help I need she's useless as a turnip. I realize that sounds horrible, but it's true. She's just different. Always has been. I love her to pieces, but she's not much help. She is a savant wine maker—better than James ever dreamed of being. I don't need to worry about quality control. As for the rest, I don't know. I do not want to think about that now. I just need to get a good night's sleep, if I can."

This time I heard, rather than saw, the defeat. "What about Morgan and Regan?" I said.

Lila glanced in their direction. They hadn't so much as glanced at their mother since I'd been paying attention. "Oh, they've got their kids," she said. "They've got their careers. You know."

I looked over to the group, the people I had lived with for twenty years while Dwight and I reared children, started the vineyard and later, the winery. Tired or not, Lila belonged with them, not sitting over here with me.

At that moment I made two decisions, one of them I would live to regret. "I just want you to know, my friend, that if you need anything, if I can do anything for you, anything at all, you need only pick up the phone." Then I stood up and walked over to the singers.

Someone had built a bonfire with wood pilfered from a stack left over from the Salmon Bake. A fresh bottle of scotch was making the rounds. I said something to Michael, and in a flash six of Lila's oldest and best friends made a beeline to our table. They picked up the wheelchair with her in it, and carried her over to the bonfire and group. Despite her fatigue, Lila actually squealed with excitement.

She was greeted with laughter and applause. The singing and storytelling resumed—a suitable wake for anyone.

CHAPTER 8

Dusk. Melody and I drove home to the Westerly. Or, rather, I drove because she had allowed her blood alcohol level to rise above the legal limit for driving. I guess that's what sober friends are for. The air was clean and soft; the western sky glowed like the bonfire we'd so recently abandoned.

"Those guys are gonna be out there until the cops find 'em and make 'em go home," Melody drawled. "And I am *drunker* than a shithouse goose." She giggled.

"You are not," I said. "You're just a little tipsy." Melody never got that drunk. She never drank more than two glasses of wine. But she may have had had three today, plus some scotch, and she's a small person. I flipped on the signal to turn left off Highway 99W and we started up the hill toward the Westerly. "At least Lila got to soak up some love."

Melody lolled back against the head rest and sighed. "Yeah, I'm just tipsy. And that's probably about all the love Lila's going to get for a while."

I shot her a look. "What's that supposed to mean? She has three daughters."

"You, who notice everything, might now comment on how close they all were actin' tonight." Melody yawned and looked away from me and toward the vineyards to our right. The undulating leaves reflected interesting, almost eerie colors as the evening darkened.

I started to answer, then shut my mouth. Melody was right. The daughters, at least the two older daughters, spent the evening talking to each other, barely noticing those who attended the memorial, much less their mother. Lila had sat at a table mostly by herself, accepting condolences of attendees, while Stephanie hung around in the background and her sisters gossiped.

"But didn't the girls make the arrangements?" I wondered.

"Morgan and Regan probably helped some. A poor event would have reflected badly on them. But Lila would have chosen the speakers and the music. She would have provided the photos for the slide show. Stephanie doesn't have any of the skills it would take to pull off an event like that and the older girls don't care. The restaurant owners stepped up. It was all their idea to take care of the food.

"You wouldn't know this since you're not out here anymore, but there was a big rift between Regan and Morgan and their dad about five years ago. They emphatically and aggressively don't care about the winery, the Ryder Estate, or anything to do with it. And they decided they didn't want anything to do with James after the fallout. I'm not sure what's at the root of that, but suffice it to say, when those two left Yamhill County, they left for good.

"Now Morgan's divorced, and guess who isn't homecoming queen anymore? Little Miss Pretty in Pink needs money. She's got a house, two kids, and a deadbeat ex. She's not meeting the type of man she's looking for in the Beaverton School District, thank you very much. And what she wants isn't looking for an overweight woman with two small children and a great big mortgage." Melody mashed a well-manicured finger against the dash for emphasis.

"Maybe her sister should show her around at the MAC Club," I said. "Isn't that where all the right people circulate?"

Melody snorted. "Maybe she has and it just didn't take, honey."

"So...." I paused a minute to let it all sink in. "So, now James is dead. From the looks of her, Lila isn't doing great—although hopefully the chemo will get her through this awful phase. Stephanie would want to continue with the winery. Yes?"

Melody nodded. "Of course. What else *can* she do? But the big girls would like to get rid of it. If Lila doesn't make it, there would be two against one. That's a big majority where I come from."

Vineyard land had been cheap from the mid-1960s into the mid-1980s. Now, in 2006, the area was enjoying boom times. Wineries were opening faster than we old-timers could ever imagine possible. Tons of money was coming into the region with no end in sight.

"If they sold today, they'd get a fortune for that estate," I said. Eighty acres, sixty-plus planted, one of the best mature vineyards in the county, would not go cheap.

I turned up the driveway to the Westerly. The air in the car was static with our thoughts, with words unspoken. I pulled the Mini up to the back deck and turned off the engine. We both sat quietly for a minute, and then Melody said, "For my money, the minute Lila is gone, old Max, wherever he is, will be up there playing kissy-kissy with Regan and Morgan, and screw poor Stephanie. When that time comes, what good will her vote be against those two?"

Now that was a twist. "Do you think he'd try to put the spa there?" I asked, horrified.

"He might, if it made sense," she said. "They have a good well, and water is the biggest issue that project faces. If Max and his cronies are able to combine the farm with their property up the hill from Ryder Estate, perhaps they could talk the commissioners into making the land use issue go away as it would be mostly farm use."

We got out of the car and walked up onto the deck. Melody pushed open the slider and Winston bounded out, sniffed us, ran around in circles, and then headed for the bushes. Melody went inside and I plopped in a deck chair. I really had been out of the loop. I'd known James and Lila for decades and always thought of the girls as children, not really a part of the decision-making process at the winery. They'd been the family. Then they all grew up and left for college, and I moved on. I'd completely forgotten about them until I saw Stephanie—now the winemaker—at the Salmon Bake, and her sisters the day after James's death.

Melody returned to the deck with two glasses and a pitcher of lemonade. She set them on the little table, went back inside, and returned with a plate of cookies and a big grin on her face. "That Angel," she said. "Look what she left for us." She poured us some lemonade and pulled up a chair for herself.

She'd gotten rid of the high heels and looked relaxed. All was quiet at the Westerly. The guests were off doing other things. Lights glowed from the pool area. Melody, queen of all she surveyed, looked settled and content. I squirmed in my chair. Her revelations about the Ryders bothered me. "It sounds like those girls are just waiting for Lila to die," I said.

Melody took a sip of her lemonade. "You got it, honey."

"Of course, that wasn't an issue until James died," I said. "If not for his murder, things would have gone along normally, I guess, at least as far as the winery was concerned. Now it's a mess."

"Yeah, but what's normal?" Melody said. "I'm real sad for Lila. They clawed, scratched, and sacrificed all those years, never two cents to rub together, then about the time things start getting easier she gets sick. 'Course nobody ever said life was fair, did they? Just look at you."

How like my dear friend to inadvertently remind me of all the past shit in my life. I took a deep breath and let it pass. We both were exhausted. I'd spent enough time around people for one day, and was about ready to retire to my suite to get away from them. Particularly if Melody was going to start in on my life and what was wrong with it.

Per usual, she didn't notice she'd hit a nerve, and blissfully plowed forward. "Oh, and you know Florian took care of my thugs for me."

To her credit, that got my attention. "How did he do that?" I said.

Melody looked at her fingernails. She was going to make me work. "He had a little talk with them," she said.

I took the bait. "Yes, Melody. I was there and saw it, remember? Do you know what he said to them?" I asked.

"As a matter of fact I do." Melody took another sip of lemonade, just making me wait until she was good and ready to tell me. She could be so damned aggravating at times. "He told the weasel that if he or any of his friends ever came near me again he would step on the guy's neck. And he meant it. How much do you know about my guest, anyway?"

Yowzer! Somehow I wasn't expecting an outright threat of violence from my friend Florian. I could have dismissed it as an empty threat, but my heart knew otherwise. As genteel a soul as he presented himself on most days, there was something about him—something private and unspoken and dangerous. "There's more to him than his public image as the bumbling Brit with the world's best wine-writing job," I told her. "But I've never been able to get anything out of him by way of specifics."

"Maybe you should try a little harder, darlin'." She winked at me. "He seems *very* protective, not to mention capable."

"No, Melody. I'm not his type, so forget that right now. You know he's after Cat." She gave me her full attention, as she hoped that by now I'd have more information on that liaison. "And no, I don't know any more about it. So, it's been such a long day I think I'll just toddle upstairs and go to bed."

Melody looked surprised, even a little hurt. Too bad. "I'd like to stay up later and gossip about Florian and Cat, however my brain is fried from this day," I said. "As for those two, you're the one who knows if he returns to the Westerly at night, so you're more in the loop than I am on those two." We'd had our little pow-wow, and she wanted to go into territory I needed to process on my own. I grabbed a couple of cookies along with my lemonade and handbag and headed for the slider. "See you in the morning," I said.

Melody put her feet up on my chair and looked as if she might make a night of it out on the deck. "Well, so far he's still sleeping out here. I'll let you know when that changes. Nighty-poo," she said as I closed the slider behind me.

I headed up the stairway, taking care to leave the door ajar so Winston could sneak up and join me later. Upstairs I carefully folded Melody's wrap, hung my dress in the closet, and slipped into my cotton jammies. I washed my face and slapped on the age-fighting and moisturizing products their manufacturer promised would keep me keep looking young and perky. Then I carefully arranged my snack on the night stand and grabbed my notebook and pen. Time to get some work done.

Some days it's just interesting to be on the planet taking it all in. This had been one of those days. Not only was it a full one from an activity standpoint, but also there were so many ripples from the proverbial pebbles dropped into the pond. For example, I liked the little ripple takeaway from Florian's encounter with the thugs. Hopefully we'd seen the last of them. But then the big question bubbled up: where was Max Weatherman? If those two had located him they wouldn't have been hanging out at James's memorial looking for him. Or, rather, looking for someone. I have a tendency to project too much, but it was safe to do so in my journal.

Then there was the business of Lila and her daughters. James's daughters. One of them had been devoted to him. But Melody had the goods—at least some of the goods—on the other two. Were the girls really nasty enough, stupid enough to avoid their parents for five years? I had no way of knowing. I'd been gone for eight years. And now, did they need money? Well, at least one of them probably did. And what had caused their rift with James in the first place? If I followed the ripples, there were enough questions upon unanswered questions to keep me up all night.

I decided I didn't have the energy. I'd made it through the memorial, and now I could go sleep. When I awoke the next morning I'd head back to Portland and find out what was going on with Florian and Cat. I closed the notebook, finished the cookies and lemonade, and brushed my teeth. I'd no sooner turned out the light when I heard little Schnauzer footsteps creeping up the stairs to my room.

CHAPTER 9

A new day dawned, as gorgeous as the one before it. Winston snored, his head on the pillow next to mine. Better than most of the men I've woken up next to. My room was bright, the air fresh and cool. Somewhere in the distance a lawnmower buzzed. I arose, donned my bathrobe, and crept down the stairs hoping to find a cup of coffee before Melody was up and about.

I was in luck. Angel banged pans in the kitchen. A carafe of coffee stood at the ready. Melody was nowhere in sight. I opened the screen and Winston dashed outside to perform his morning ablutions.

Angel noticed me as I poured a cup of coffee. "Good morning, Senora," she said.

"Hi Angel, how's it going?" I carried my coffee over to the oak table and sat down.

She plopped something on a small plate and set it in front of me. "I try something new today," she said. "I want your opinion."

I examined the small, puffy pastry that had been dusted with powdered sugar, and then bit into it. A delicious custardy filling squirted out both sides. I managed to catch the escaped filling and propel it into my mouth. Creamy, buttery, eggy, not too sweet. Just the right amount of vanilla. "Wow, Angel, what is it?"

Angel smiled and rubbed her hands on her apron. "I experiment with the Mexican pastries, Senora. It is what you call the adaptation?"

"Keep adapting," I said. "I'm all for it!" Angel bowed her head, her face flushed with pleasure.

Melody entered the room, also in her bathrobe. "What's goin' on in here?" she said as she poured herself a cup of coffee.

"And good morning to you, too," I said. "Angel is experimenting."

Melody walked over to the sheet of fresh pastries and carefully inspected them. She helped herself to one, and took a big bite. "Umm-mm!" She smacked her lips, and advanced to the table, pastry in hand. She sat, took a sip of her coffee, and then fixed me with a beady stare. "And don't you think for a second that I don't know about you and that stinkin' dog," she said. "All over my expensive bedding. I've been up for an hour and I *know* he was not down here where he shoulda been."

Damn. Busted. "It's not his fault," I said.

"Bull*shit!*" Melody said. "You don't think he didn't spend weeks goin' up there every day and lookin' for you after you went home last fall?" She paused for dramatic effect, then took another bite of the pastry. "But I have bigger fish to fry today," she continued. "I'm heading over to visit Lila this morning. I'd like you to come with me."

Oh, would you. I thought about it for less than half a second. I'd had enough of the dead and dying to last me a good long while. "No thanks," I said. "I'm planning to take Winston for a walk, if you don't mind, and then head back to Portland."

Again I was treated to one of her looks. "Suit yourself," she said. "But Lila is going to need a lot of support in the coming months."

"I'm completely aware of that," I said. "And she has many capable and generous friends such as yourself to see her through this time. I need to be in Portland today."

Melody glanced over her shoulder at Angel, who was working on breakfast for the paying guests. Then she looked back at me. I felt as if I was watching a rattlesnake coiled and ready to strike. "You could be a big help to her," she said.

I jumped in before she could follow her line of thought any further. "You know, Melody, Lila is a grownup. She's dealt with big issues all her life, and she's dealt with them pretty well. I'd say that she and her family and close friends are up to these current challenges as well as anyone else. I am not her best friend. I've been out of her life for a long time."

"I'm just sayin'...."

"I know where you're going with this. You mean well," I said, "but this is not your business. I told her to call me if I could help in any way, and I meant it. But right now, today, I'm going home. I need to go to my AA meeting tonight. I have stuff to do to keep my own life on track. You do what you need to do as long as it doesn't involve me."

Melody for once said nothing. Her disapproving look said enough. I'd endured those looks for many years and they hadn't killed me yet. I waited her out.

Finally she sighed. "Go in peace," she said.

I felt a surge of relief. "Thanks for understanding," I said. An hour later I was in my car headed back to Lower Hillsdale Heights.

CHAPTER 10

Back at my cozy bungalow, I hand-watered the garden and took a nap. For dinner I made a simple pasta with fresh tomatoes, olive oil, Kalamata olives, garlic, and basil. And then I hauled my sorry ass to the Sunday evening AA meeting located in a nearby church basement. I didn't speak at the meeting. Instead, this time I just soaked up the message of recovery and hope and then visited with my friends after the meeting. It restored my sense of balance, which had been thrown out of whack by the past week's events. Thank goodness for AA meetings. I don't know how normal people survive.

At home, I watched a mystery program on television and turned in early. For the moment I was well-fed, peaceful, and content. My life is pretty simple most of the time.

Monday morning I woke up early, completely refreshed. I downed a cup of coffee, then set out on a vigorous walk that once again took me to Council Crest Park, the Sacajawea statue, and breathtaking views to the east of Portland and Mt. Hood. The long uphill hike had gotten my heart rate up and left me feeling cleansed.

I drank from my water bottle and sat for a while before heading back down the hill to home.

There I booted up my laptop, answered some emails, and paid a couple of bills. My meager funds were at a historic low, and yet the quest to find a job that utilized what I knew were my aptitudes and skills eluded me. On days like this, alone and discouraged, I truly wondered what would become of me.

After a late lunch, I collapsed on the sofa in a funk. A nap, I figured, would clear my brain enough to carry me through into the evening. Obviously I needed to be grateful for what I had. I planned to call Cat later and learn what joy she might have to share.

My phone woke me from a deep sleep. I grabbed for it, not knowing whether it was day or night. "Hello?" I sounded vacant, confused. I looked at my watch. It was nearly five.

"Is this Emma Golden?" The voice on the phone sounded equally confused.

"It is." I paused to gather my wits. "Who's this?"

"Hi Emma, this is Lila Ryder. Is this a good time to talk?"

At the moment, I did have time. Plenty of time. "Sure Lila, how are you doing today?"

Lila sounded down even more than she had at James's memorial. "You asked if you could help me, right? Did you mean it?"

I steeled myself, all the while telling myself it would be something ridiculously simple. "Of course I did," I said. "You know I'll do anything I'm able. What do you need?"

Lila's voice caught as she resumed speaking. "I'm having a rough time." She took a deep breath. "I'm by myself here at the house, and I fell today. I can't be here alone. I need somebody to stay with me for a week or two. Just until I can figure out what I'm going to do next. I've been so confused by all this upheaval...." Her voice trailed off. In the distance that separated us I heard the catch of a sob, and then she said, "Could you come out here and stay with me? Just for a few days?"

Sadness threatened to overwhelm me. It was bad enough she had cancer and had just lost the love of her life, but that Lila—a woman with three living children—had to ask someone like me, someone she hadn't connected with in more than eight years, to come out and be her companion. What was wrong with this picture? Where were those daughters? It wasn't exactly the kind of thing I could ask her.

Still, the request floored me. I tried to not pause before answering. "OK, Lila," I said, as I let the weight of her request and its ramifications sink in. "Talk to me about this. What, specifically, do you need from me?"

A sniff from the neighboring county. Her voice wispy, she talked brokenly. I could almost feel the tears that no doubt were running down her face as she tried to speak normally. "Oh, Emma, I am so sorry. It's hard to have to ask someone like this, but I don't know what else I can do. I need someone to be here overnight. After that fall, I don't feel safe by being myself. I'm having chemo at the end of the week, and it's always super difficult for a few days after that. I just thought of you and hoped you'd have the time to help me."

I had to force myself to not ask about the daughters. I said, "It's all right, Lila. I'd be happy to help for a few days. What kind of things will you need me to do while I'm there?"

Her voice broke. "Oh, I hate this." Another sniff and a deep breath. "At times I need help just to get up and go to the bathroom. I'm having trouble organizing my medications. I need to be sure to take them on time. Hopefully, you could take me over to St. Vincent on Friday for chemo. And then someone needs to be around when I take a shower. That sort of thing."

I hoped to God I wouldn't be asked to scrub anything! Ideally it wouldn't get *too* personal. I'm not the kind of person most people would want for a caregiver. Even so, I'd made up my mind in a heartbeat, because if she was asking me she must really be desperate. Where were all those lifelong friends? I wasn't doing anything that couldn't wait a few days, and the poor woman was in a crisis. "Sure, Lila, don't worry about a thing. When do you want me there?"

"Really? Oh my God, thank you." Lila started all-out crying. I waited silently for her to compose herself. "I don't know what else I would have done short of hiring a complete stranger." Now that was bad. "It feels almost like a miracle that you'll do this," she continued. "I'm so grateful I listened to Melody."

Melody! "I beg your pardon?" I said. I tried to keep my voice neutral. I could hear Melody telling me, "You could be a big help to her." Yeah. Right.

"She came by this morning," Lila said. "I just didn't know what I was going to do, and she suggested you might have some time to help."

"I'm happy to help, Lila," I said, and I meant it even though my jaw was clenched. "We'll do just fine, I promise."

"I am so relieved. Come out as soon as you can. I'll make sure the guest room is all ready for you."

"Don't be trying to do any of that yourself," I said. "I'll be out tomorrow late morning, and I can certainly make a bed."

After we disconnected, I began making a list. What did I need to do before I left my place for an unknown number of days? What could I take with me that would help me and engage Lila? Scrabble board? Books? How much work was this really going to be? Well, it didn't matter. I had signed on. Other people weren't available for whatever multitude of reasons, and Melody had directed Lila toward me.

I dialed Melody's cell phone. She picked up on the first ring. "How could you do that?" I demanded, skipping the niceties.

Melody was all innocence. "What on *earth* do you mean?"

"Cut it out, Melody. You sicced Lila on me. "

"Now just a short minute." I could almost see Melody puffing up for battle. "Did you or did you not tell me that you asked our mutual friend if there was anything you could do to help? All she needed to do was call you, am I right?"

"I'm happy to help her. What I find objectionable is your part in it."

"Well, dear, consider it this way: you were looking for a job and now you have one."

More justifying. I wanted to smack her. "You know what I mean. I'm happy to stay with her for a couple of days, but not weeks. I don't want to get stuck out there. I have a life, and it's in Portland. But the biggest issue is that I am not a caregiver. Never have been. Never wanted to be."

Melody continued, unruffled. "Does that mean you said yes?"

"Of course I said yes. What else would I do? The poor woman. But this could get out of my comfort zone really fast. You of all people know that!"

"Oh, calm down," she said. "You had babies, you cleaned their little bottoms. They puked on you. You'll be fine."

That was not the response I wanted to hear. Companionship was one thing; bodily functions were quite another. "I know your intentions are good," I said. "The part I don't like is you interfering in my life, setting me up for something like this without even including me in the process."

Never missing a beat, Melody said, "Well, we can't always choose where we're needed, now, can we."

"Since you're so confident about what people need, why didn't you go up there to stay with her?" I said. "I don't see you volunteering for anything."

"Well," she replied. "I already have a job, don't I."

I hung up on her. The truth was, if she'd suggested I volunteer to help Lila in some capacity that hadn't occurred to me, I probably would have. Instead, she took the path that caught me unawares and backed me into a corner. I felt like a pawn being moved around on a chess board. While I'd managed to let off a little steam, I still felt Melody had used me—even though I was willing and able to be useful.

CHAPTER 11

That evening I called Cat. She was just leaving to meet Florian downtown for drinks. Did I want to join them?

"What? Sit around and watch you guys drink and make calf eyes? Hell no," I said. Then I asked her if they were seeing each other every day. They were. I thought so. I asked her to water my garden while I was gone. She agreed. I packed a suitcase and turned in early.

The next morning promised another day of perfect Pacific Northwest summer weather. It was one of those days when a person just wants to go out and roll in the grass naked somewhere. At least my mind traveled in those directions. Then I played the tape to the end. Not a great idea. I'd probably get arrested. But I could, since I was planning a trip to another county, stop at a fruit stand and purchase some wonderful Willamette Valley peaches and eat them until I got goofy on the juice.

I loaded the car. There wasn't that much to take. I wasn't moving, I was driving forty miles. I could always come back and take a break if I needed to. I did bring my laptop in case any interesting jobs turned up on line. I needed to get out of the financial rut I was in.

On the way to the Ryder Estate I stopped to see Melody. I wanted her to feel my full displeasure regarding her meddling. Breakfast was just ending as I stepped into the kitchen. I hugged Angel and helped myself to a cup of coffee.

Melody bustled in from the dining room, basket of scones in hand. She looked a little surprised to see me. "Well, good morning to you, too," she said.

I treated her to my brightest smile. "Top o' the top of the morning, you old sage hen." I made myself comfortable at the round table.

Melody sat down across from me. "You're out and about early."

"Yes," I said, "I'm out here to fulfill my duties. You know, that babysitting job you set up for me."

Melody smacked her hand down on the table. "Lila needs your help. Get over it," she said.

I took a sip of coffee and ignored the theatrics. "This is not about me and Lila, Melody. This is about me and *you*. Make your own plans, not mine. It's that simple."

Melody managed to put on her hurt look. "I was only trying to help."

"Don't act all innocent," I said. "There's more to it than that because we keep having this same conversation. Can't you just quit? I don't need a parent, I just need a friend for godssakes."

Melody sighed. She rested her hands in her lap and looked me in the eye. "I guess I can try," she said. "I'll really try. That's all I can promise right now."

I nodded. "I'll take it," I said. "Just be aware, okay? Friend. Not. Parent. You've got kids. Parent them."

"They won't let me." Melody laughed her deep, throaty laugh. "They both moved out of the state to get away from me."

I chuckled and shook my head. Alas, it was all too true. "Well, there you go," I said. "I'm not leaving the state. But I do want to be able to pick up the phone when you call and not wonder what you're going to do to improve my life for me. I'm just trying to be honest here, not to hurt your feelings."

"All right, now let's talk about something else," she said.

I thought for a moment, then said, "What about Max Weatherman? Has he showed his face?"

"Isn't that the weirdest thing?" Melody said. "He hasn't come near here. Florian is busy visiting wineries, of course, and he's been doin' a little askin' around. Nary a peep. Nobody he's talked to has seen a sign of our friend Max. And I've still got all his shit in the basement."

I thought briefly about making another trip to the Pearl. My ability to learn anything from lurking around his condo was limited at best. "It amazes me that anyone as visible as he's made himself over the last little while can just disappear completely," I mused.

"Well, he's gone, and I presume the thugs are out of here as well. At least I can sleep since Florian had his little come-to-Jesus with them."

I took a final sip of now-tepid coffee. "Well, it's time for me to get moving. I need to get out of here and see what I can do for Lila."

I drove slowly through the vineyards to the Ryder Estate. For vineyard workers, this was the time of year to cut back foliage on the grapevines. The pros call it canopy management. Not only did this expose the grapes to more sunshine for better ripening, but also enabled the plants to put more of their energy into grape development rather than leaf development. Most vineyards had permanent crews for all the tasks that needed to be done throughout the year. Extra workers were hired during harvest, and went on to other agricultural jobs during the remainder of the growing season. Many wintered at their homes in Mexico.

When I pulled up to the Ryder home—I couldn't bear to think of it as Lila's place just yet—it was just past eleven. I grabbed my bag from the back seat and walked up to the door. It was ajar, so I hit the doorbell and then saw myself in. I removed my shoes just inside the door and walked barefoot across polished wood into the living room. "Lila?" I called. "It's Emma. Where are you?"

"Over here, Emma. Come on in."

I walked to the dining room and glanced to my right. She was standing behind the bar in the open kitchen, apparently working at a counter. "What are you doing walking around?" I blurted. It never occurred to me that I'd find her on her feet. I set my bag down and walked closer to the bar.

Lila looked up from her task and smiled. Standing, her thinness was remarkable. Her skin, which hung on her, was an unhealthy pasty hue. "Oh, I'm having a pretty good day, actually. I thought I'd do a few things in here while I'm feeling okay," she said. "You know what they say: You can sleep when you're dead." She chuckled.

I didn't find her remark the least bit funny. "That's great, just don't overdo," I said. "I mean, isn't that why I'm here? To help you?"

She grimaced. "Oh, you'll get to do plenty of that. I have chemo on Friday. And thank you so much for coming. I've been looking forward to having the company."

I moseyed around the bar and into the kitchen. "Where are the glasses? I need a drink of water."

Lila pointed to a cabinet. I opened it, selected a glass, and filled it at the tap. She was working determinedly on something, and when I moved next to her I saw she was trying to remove the peel from some slices of cantaloupe. Little beads of perspiration had gathered on her brow. "Why don't you let me do that?" I said. "It's getting to be lunch time. What would you like me to fix you?"

Lila relinquished the paring knife she'd been using and moved around the counter. She climbed onto a stool and sat at the bar. "I guess I have been standing a bit longer than I should," she said. "There's some chicken in the fridge. A slice of cold chicken would be nice."

Maybe, but it didn't float my boat. I opened the refrigerator and began rummaging. I emerged with several ingredients and mixed up some chicken salad. Then I hollowed out two of the large, ripe tomatoes I found on the counter and filled them with the salad.

Lila watched silently. But when I set a plate in front of her and said, "Voila!" she clapped her hands in delight. "If this is how you're going to take care of me I'll keep you here forever," she said.

Please God, not that, I thought. But I did feel warm and fuzzy. Cooking for people seems to bring out the best in me. I pulled up the stool next to Lila at the bar.

We ate and chit-chatted. Rather, I ate. Lila picked. Our conversation ran along very safe lines. What my daughter was doing on the East Coast running somebody's art gallery. The relative merits of the 2005 harvest over previous years. Snippets of wine industry gossip. My mind strayed. How on earth was I going to *do* this for a week or even two and keep my marbles? It was going to be boring. And where *was* Max Weatherman, anyway? Well, one could always ask, and I did, more to entertain myself than with any expectation of receiving an answer.

When I mentioned his name, Lila straightened her back and looked at me, eyes flashing. "Yes, as a matter of fact, I did see Max Weatherman," Lila said. "About a week before James died he came out here just as I was preparing to take a nap. He wanted to talk about his spa plans. James wasn't home, and I sent him on his way. I let those discussions go on when I'm not present. They upset me too much. James handles—handled—everything to do with Mr. Weatherman."

"Has he been by since?" I asked. "I mean, neighbor paying respects, that sort of thing."

Lila shot me a look. "He better *not* come back here," she said. "I don't need respects from that man. As far as I'm concerned, he's a murderer."

Well, a hot button. But it also told me she didn't know he'd gone missing. How could she? She'd had so much to deal with over the past ten days it was unimaginable. I had all kinds of questions I wanted to ask her. Most of them could wait. It wouldn't be polite to start bombarding the poor women all at once. But I really was curious about the daughters, and Lila's plans for the future of the winery. No polite way to ask those questions right now, and I knew it.

I began tidying up from lunch. Dishes in the dishwasher, items returned to the refrigerator. I wanted to learn the landscape of the kitchen as quickly as possible. It was a great kitchen in terms of both design and function, but somewhere in it or near it there lurked an odor. It was faint but nasty. Maybe something in the garbage disposal. Or, perhaps I needed to empty the garbage and that would take care of it.

Lila sat at the bar watching me and sipping iced tea. She looked sad. As I was finishing up she said, "I'm going to go take a nap. I'll be out of touch for a couple of hours."

"Sounds good," I said. "What do you want for dinner?" Based on the lunch she'd consumed, it wouldn't be very much.

She considered it for a moment. "Oh, I don't care," she said. "Surprise me." She got to her feet and gestured. "Come with me and I'll show you to your room."

She began walking through the living room. I grabbed my bag off the floor and followed her down a long hallway. My room—beautiful, with a private bath—was at the end of a significant hallway. "It seems like I'm a very long way from where you'll be," I said.

Lila smiled. "You'll love this room," she said. "If you're going out today, you can pick up a baby monitor at Fred Meyer. Or not. I'm not worried. If I need you, my lungs still work pretty well."

Borderline gallows humor. It did, however, offer me a break. I said, "Sure, I can do that. I'll go now while you're resting."

Back in the living room, I sat on the fabulous flocked settee while Lila went into the bedroom. I ran my hand over the upholstery, savoring the beauty of the piece of furniture, the surrounding art, the room in general.

Lila came out of her bedroom and pressed a debit card into my hand, along with a slip of paper. "This will cover the purchases," she said. She told me the PIN code for the card and wiggled the slip of paper. "You'll need to pick up a prescription for me along with the list of the things I need."

"Great, I'll take care of it."

She disappeared into the master suite and closed the door. I retrieved a few more things from the car and carried them down to my room. I unpacked. There wasn't much to do. Once it was done I stood at the large window and looked out over the vineyard. Lush and perfect green rows interspersed with terra-cotta colored soil cascaded downward to the south. It was almost two o'clock and quite warm, but the workers in their long-sleeved shirts and straw hats continued their tasks, moving slowly downhill between the rows.

Inside the temperature was a comfortable, air-conditioned level. I looked around the room. Nice art on the walls, mostly local artists. Thick, fluffy towels in the bathroom. I arranged my beauty products and admired the stone walk-in shower. And a new HD television. I didn't have a TV in my suite at Melody's. I might get caught up on some movies during my stay. It's not likely I'd be out running around socializing at night.

Everything was perfect, but I realized I did not feel at ease. I felt like a maid. The truth was that with Lila I felt a bit like a stranger. I had always liked and admired her, but from a distance. Because of our roles in the industry it was James I'd been close to. I'd call him with questions. He'd call me with tips. When we saw each other, we'd put our heads together to discuss the ins and outs of a situation. It was fun and enlightening. I knew him and it had been an easy friendship.

Lila, for me, had been part of the background. So what was I doing here? Well, thanks to Melody and to my inability to say no and offer some alternative to help Lila, I was going to be a caregiver. I knew she had household help. Lucila, Angel's cousin, showed up a couple days a week to keep the house looking lovely. But I was the one who'd get stuck with the intimate stuff if it came to that. I hoped it wouldn't. If it did, I'd have to deal with it, and it was my own damn fault. I only planned to stay long enough for her to make other arrangements.

I knew I would get through it, no matter what. So right then and there, I vowed I'd make the best of it. If Lila slept like a log during the afternoons, I could go over to the Westerly and hang out by the pool. Florian was still around. Maybe I could even take some time to ride shotgun with him to some of his interviews. That would be fun. And, I might even figure out what the hell had happened to Max Weatherman—if, indeed, anything had happened at all. Maybe he had gone back to Nevada to chill and talk it over with his financial backers. That made a lot of sense to me.

I walked out to my car and started the engine. Something niggled me. Weatherman was still around here somewhere. I just didn't know where yet. With so many people looking for him, someone was certain to find him soon enough.

Even mid-afternoon on a weekday the Highway 99 traffic was heavy—particularly through Dundee, where the highway narrowed to two lanes. I drove slowly, keeping pace with lumbering motor homes, logging trucks, and general traffic. It took half an hour to get to the east side of Newberg where the Fred Meyer is located. I found a parking spot and sat for a moment drinking water from my bottle. On an impulse, I pulled out my phone and called Rob Grimes. He answered on the first ring.

I identified myself and cut to the chase. "Have the police located Max Weatherman yet?" I asked. "I just remembered they came out to the Westerly last week to question him."

"I'm not in my office. Hang on a second." I waited until Rob finished doing whatever it was he was doing. "I'm back, and the answer to your question is no. I was over at the sheriff's office earlier today and read the latest reports. They were able to check his condo in the Pearl and there's no sign of him. He hasn't been there for a while. Food was rotting in the refrigerator."

"Do they have any idea where he is? Do they think he went back to Henderson?"

"Nooo...." Rob was on his computer or something. And then he was back again. "They don't know where he might be. They checked with his wife and she hasn't heard from him in more than a week."

Wife? Now that was news to me. But people actually did have them. "Where's the wife?" I said. "Here or Henderson?"

"Oh, she lives in Henderson. Or they do. His condo up here is supposedly a temporary situation."

I thought of the younger woman the old sleaze was chasing at the Salmon Bake. "Wasn't the wife concerned when she didn't hear from him?"

"Well, I guess not, until after the deputies got through with her. She was a little pissed off that he'd been gone so long, and they hadn't been talking much. But now, according to Jeffers, she's all shook, as you might imagine."

"Understandably." I thought for a moment. "Well, thanks Rob. I'm out here now for a few days helping Lila Ryder, so let's keep in touch. He may still be off stage pulling some strings. I just hope he doesn't show up here and get Lila all upset."

"Got it," said Rob. "I'll be checking in with the commissioners this week regarding his applications for variance. If he's around they've no doubt heard from him.

"And speaking of Mrs. Ryder," he continued, "you should probably know that an expensive eight-inch Japanese chef's knife is missing from her knife drawer."

The guy's losing his marbles, I thought. "So what?" I said.

"It's the same knife that was used to stab James Ryder."

I let it sink in. "Oh, shit," I said finally. "What does that mean?"

"What it means," said Rob, "is that they took her passport and told her not to leave town. Nobody really thinks she did anything, given her illness and all. But someone got hold of that knife. It has a very sharp tip. You should see the sucker."

My stomach churned just thinking about it. "I know what those knives are like," I said. "It's sickening."

"Yeah, well, while we're talking passports, they also took Stephanie's."

Stephanie. "Her father was her hero," I said.

I could hear Rob shuffling papers at the other end of the line. "You know they really grill family members when something like this happens," he said. "They've spent hours with each one of them. Apparently the other two daughters were nowhere near Yamhill County the night of the murder."

We hung up. When someone is nosy, it's cool to have a Rob in your life. A lot of people were wondering where Max Weatherman had gone, myself included. While I didn't really have a dog in the fight, it was fun to speculate. Rob had access to places where I didn't, so I'd definitely keep in touch. Weatherman could be the link to what had happened to James. Maybe he was just holed up with a woman somewhere out here in the boonies. But I didn't think so. People usually came up for air after three or four days.

Still, if he didn't talk to his wife much, who'd know the difference? And how would he know people were looking for him if he was in some isolated love nest—either here or Portland, or even at the coast? If he still was around here, and courting, surely they would have showed up at a restaurant or somewhere else where they'd be seen and recognized. Something smelled rotten in Yamhill

County. Now that I was here and in need of distraction, perhaps I would learn what it was. Without actually interfering, of course.

So what about that knife? I thought about that all the way through the errands, plus another bumper-to-bumper drive through Newberg and Dundee, which took much longer than I'd anticipated. It was Lila's knife. She'd had access to it. She could stand. She could walk. She was a suspect. How likely a suspect I had no way of knowing.

Could she, would she kill? If so, why? Had James been unfaithful? Were there money problems? Had she gone nuts? More to the point, was I taking care of a murderer? I couldn't imagine Lila killing James. But it gave me a lot to consider. Should I be concerned for my own safety? My intuition said no. It didn't wash.

It was nearly five when I pulled in at the Ryder home. Lila's house. Whatever. I hauled three large bags of groceries into the house, which was cool and silent as a stone. The door to the master bedroom was still closed. I figured Lila was resting, and decided to just let her rest for a bit longer. If it seemed like too long, I'd check. But for now I could enjoy the peace.

I unpacked groceries, further familiarizing myself with the kitchen. Yes, it was a fine kitchen. I could make myself right at home there. Fancy gas stove, two ovens, and a cute little gas grill built into a wall like a fireplace. I was practically beside myself with that feature. Since I'd found some lamb chops for dinner, I could get right to work figuring out how it worked.

To further familiarize myself, I located the knife drawer. It stocked a great number of very good knives. There was one for every conceivable culinary purpose, I was convinced. And yes, one was noticeably missing from its slot. I shut the drawer. It was difficult to wrap my mind around the possibility that the murder weapon had come from the Ryders' very own kitchen.

To distract myself, I took another look at the built-in grill. I stuck my head into the grilling space to check out the ventilation system. Something moved behind me. Alarmed, I jumped and hit my head before pulling it out of the space. I looked behind me to see Lila. I caught my breath. My heart pounded. Suddenly I felt shaky. "Hey sunshine," I said, feigning a calmness I didn't feel. "Are you getting hungry?"

I gave her the once over. Was she a murderer? She didn't look like one, but what did I know? She did look like hell, pale and drawn under her red wig. She also looked as if she'd been crying. What did I expect? She'd just lost her husband. "No thanks," she said. "Not yet." Her hands gripped her arms as if she was cold. She walked around to where I was standing. "This was James's idea," she said.

I nodded. "Yeah, it's really cool. I'm going to grill us some lamb chops in it this evening if you'll show me how it works."

Lila stuck her head into the space. I thought briefly of Sylvia Plath. "I will, if I can remember," she said, pulling her head out. "I'll probably be able to get something down in a couple hours. Right now I just need something to drink." She shrugged. "I just don't know what."

"Go sit down and I'll see what we've got." I opened the refrigerator and began exploring. I finally settled on some Perrier with cranberry juice. If she didn't want it, I'd drink it. Meanwhile I was happy with water. And there would be food. Hopefully Lila would be able to eat it.

My gaze fell upon a tray of prescriptions next to the refrigerator. I held up each one and read the directions. Two bottles indicated doses four times a day. We'd missed at least one. I carried the tray out to where Lila sat and handed her the drink I'd prepared. I set the tray on a small table next to her. "Okay, what about this stuff?" I asked.

Lila gave it a dismissive look. "What about it?"

I held up the two bottles of pills. I hadn't even looked at the rest. "Did you take these when you were supposed to before I got here?"

Lila looked confused. "Uh…I think I took them this morning."

"You think?"

"Well, yes. I mean, I'm not completely certain, but I think I did. Yes. I did."

She didn't know if she'd taken them or not. She took a sip of the cranberry concoction and set it down. "Not bad." She nodded at me.

I was going through the rest of the pill bottles. It was a rat maze. I looked up. "Did you take them at lunch time? No, because I was here." I read the labels, shook out one of each, and placed them in her hand. "Here, take them now."

She took the pills.

"It says 'with food'," I said. "Do you have any crackers?"

Lila pointed in the direction of a cabinet. I got up and found the crackers. I also grabbed the small notepad next to the telephone. I handed her the package of crackers and sat back down. "We need a system."

Lila nodded. She nibbled a cracker without enthusiasm.

"At least I need a system," I said.

"I guess that's why you're here," she said. "I can't seem to remember things."

I rearranged the bottles of pills into four categories: morning, noon, evening, and bedtime. Then I started making notes. "It's a wonder you remember what day it is, after all that's happened," I said. "Eat some more of those crackers."

"I'm not hungry."

I wasn't in the mood. "Eat them anyway," I said. "Otherwise those pills will tear your guts out. You have enough problems without getting sick on your medications."

Lila reluctantly stuck her hand back into the cracker box and pulled out a couple more. At the rate she was going, it would take her all night to eat a few crackers. She took a sip of the cranberry juice cocktail and grimaced. "You're a pill Nazi," she said.

"Sometimes this stuff works if you take it like you're supposed to," I said. I bundled up the pill bottles, placed my written instructions on the tray with them, and carried them back into the kitchen.

Dinner was only a small disaster. I chowed down three grilled lamb chops plus two helpings of the radicchio salad I had made to accompany, and some wonderful grilled bread slathered in butter. Lila took her pills, then moved food around on her plate, picked, and managed about three bites. I had anticipated a situation of this sort, and had picked up a pint of Ben & Jerry's ice cream, plus fresh berries from a roadside stand, during my afternoon errands. I dished up a large helping of the ice cream for her and topped it with raspberries and blueberries.

Lila managed a smile. "Oh, this looks lovely!" she said. She tucked into the ice cream and ate the whole thing. Once she was settled in her favorite chair, I made us each a double decaf espresso. We adjourned to the deck to watch the sunset and sip coffee. We chatted for a bit about some bygone events, but mostly just sat quietly. The evening birds came out and zipped through the vineyard and flower beds. A doe and two fawns meandered between two rows of grapes nibbling new shoots off the vines. In the fading light, I even noticed bats coming out to feed.

By nine, the sun was down and Lila was ready for bed. I had to admit that I was tired, too. She showed me her evening ritual—she could do everything in terms of personal care. I set out her medications, watched her swallow them, then said goodnight and headed to my room. It had been a long day.

I was just changing into my pajamas when my phone rang. Rob. I hit the talk button. "What's up?"

"They found Weatherman's BMW."

"Wow. Where?"

"It went over an embankment up on Bald Peak."

I had to process that for a moment. The visuals, the possibilities. "What about Weatherman?" I asked. "Is he dead?"

Rob sighed. "Here's the deal," he said. "There was nobody in the vehicle. There was nobody even *near* it. The car was spotted by a local about three this afternoon, and deputies have been combing the area since then. Nothing. No body, no blood, no nothing. Just an empty, totaled car. They think it went over the embankment empty. So the question remains, where is Max Weatherman?"

My mind was having a field day, but "Oh crap," was the only thing I could think of to say. I paused for a moment. "Now what?"

"I guess we wait," said Rob. "I filed my story and just got home a few minutes ago, so that is all for now."

We disconnected. I walked over to my window and stared out over the darkened fields toward the Coast Range. It occurred to me that the goons from Nevada may have caught up with Max Weatherman. Or maybe he pulled this stunt himself just to get people off his tail. Or any number of other possibilities that hadn't yet crossed my mind. I'd probably need to have coffee with Melody in the morning to get her up to speed and see what she thought. In the meantime, I had my trusty notebook. I pulled it out of my bag, threw it on the bed, and repaired to the bathroom for evening ablutions with beauty products. Then I crawled into what turned out to be a very comfortable bed and began writing.

CHAPTER 12

I awakened to a pale sky streaked with red. It was early—much earlier than I am given to rising—but I'd gone to sleep a couple hours earlier than normal. I was ready for the day.

All was calm in the house of the rising sun. I padded down the hall, through the living room, and into the gorgeous kitchen, where I set about making a pot of coffee. I had cased the place sufficiently the day before to know where all the coffee equipment was kept. It took only a moment to get things going. Then I lightly tapped and then opened Lila's door and peeped inside. She was sound asleep and breathing regularly.

Back in my room, I showered. Then I donned lightweight slacks and a tee shirt and walking shoes. By the time I'd dressed, the coffee was done. I poured myself a mug and headed outside onto the deck. The house was stuffy and still smelled weird, so I left the doors wide open to air out the living room-dining room area.

I couldn't remain on the deck for long. The vineyard foliage, iridescent in the early morning light, undulated in the very slight breeze. It beckoned and I couldn't resist. I topped off my mug and headed down the stairs leading from the deck to the back yard and into the vines. I meandered down the hill between the rows. Up the hill behind me I heard the voices of men calling to each other in Spanish. The workday was beginning for the field workers, but I still had a few minutes to enjoy myself amongst the vines.

It was a comforting feeling wherein I felt at home and at peace. I remembered walking the vineyard with James many years ago, before the bottom half of the property even had been planted. He'd been so full of life and enthusiasm. With him gone, what would happen to the estate? Lila's future was uncertain at best. Among the three daughters, one was a big city lawyer, the other a teacher. Only Stephanie, as winemaker, had shown any interest in its ongoing success. And where was she? She lived out here somewhere near the winery. I knew that much, but little more. It was ten or twelve years since I'd had a conversation with her, and back then she'd been in high school. How time flew!

If I was going to be hanging around here, that was going to change. Like today. Those girls needed to know that I wasn't moving in with their mom. Given her illness, I didn't know how pro-active Lila wanted to be or even could be. Obviously the chemo was kicking her butt. She didn't feel like eating much, and apparently spent a lot of time sleeping. So maybe one of the things I could do to help was to ensure she had more permanent care so I could go home and live my life, sooner rather than later. The daughters' involvement was imperative.

Uphill somewhere a tractor motor started with a familiar rumbling roar. I turned and started back toward the house. As I neared the deck, I saw the tractor lumbering down the far side of the vineyard, sprayers blasting. Copper-sulfate was sprayed to deter the growth of powdery mildew. A miracle substance for grape growers, it also had the advantages of being organic and bio-degradable, but it was not a good idea to inhale while it was being applied. The tractor driver wore a mask. I bounded up the steps and into the living room, closing the doors tightly behind me.

By the time Lila arose around eight-thirty, I'd already devoured the newspaper and was ready to roll. She ate a bit of scrambled egg, nibbled some toast, and drank a glass of fresh-squeezed orange juice. I lined up her meds and watched her swallow them, and then it was off to the shower. I sat outside the bathroom door and worked the Sudoku puzzle, thankful that for now my presence wasn't required within.

By nine-thirty I was bored to near screaming. "Is there anything you need to do today?" I inquired after Lila was dressed and seated in her chair overlooking the vineyard. The sprayers were still at it.

She sighed and turned over the book on the table hear her—the book she hadn't been reading. "Nothing in particular."

"What do you need me to do for you?"

She shrugged. "Nothing, really. Lucila will be here any minute, so she'll take care of everything in the kitchen, do the laundry and whatever else needs to be taken care of around the house. To tell you the truth, that's about as much as I can deal with." She shook her head in frustration and the red hair that once belonged to someone else swung attractively around her face. Once again I caught the sadness in her voice, and in her general demeanor.

Dammit! "OK," I began, wracking my brain to figure out what to do for the next two hours. "Are you feeling up for a drive?"

Lila brightened a bit. "Sure, that might be fun."

"Jiggling in the car won't bother you?" I asked. "I'd like to do some exploring and we might be on some gravel roads."

"Oh, I'm fine. That sounds wonderful. I'll just leave a note for Lucila."

Fifteen minutes later we found ourselves in Lila's red BMW sedan, me in the driver's seat. Gravel or no, this vehicle didn't jiggle or jolt its passengers. I headed straight for Bald Peak. I am such a slut for gossip—or information of the more titillating persuasion. I just had to see where Max Weatherman's car had gone off the road, just because. It drove me crazy that nobody could find that man.

Bald Peak is the highest peak in Yamhill County and boasts amazing views of just about everything. It can be a dangerous, curvy drive in the dark or in bad weather, so it is never surprising when a vehicle goes off the road. However, this was full summer. Thus, the incident with Weatherman's sports car had been deemed suspicious. As we neared the top of the hill, on a very tight curve, I spotted the place the car had gone over. Yellow tape ran along the road for 50 feet or so in either direction.

I slowed the car to a crawl. Fortunately nobody was behind me. "Oh my," I said. "Somebody missed a curve."

Lila craned her neck to look at the disturbance. "How awful," she said. "I hope no one got hurt."

I wanted to get out and look around, but couldn't figure out a good enough reason to do so. There was no place to pull off the road, adding another wet blanket to the plan. So I continued the drive up to the state park. At the summit, I parked the car and we both got out. Lila was a little shaky, but with my assistance she managed to walk to the best viewpoint and take in the breathtaking panorama of the valley, green checkerboard farmland, and the Coast Range showing its layers of deep, cool colors.

Back in the car she said, "Thank you. I haven't been up here for *years*. I'd forgotten it was here. I used to bring the girls up here for a picnic on the hottest days, before we had air-conditioning."

I just nodded. "Sometimes we forget the treasures nearest us," I said. We wound down the hill and headed back toward the small city of Yamhill, where we stopped for ice cream cones.

We sat in the car eating them. Lila appeared relaxed and cheerful, and was even enjoying the ice cream. Once again, I tried to imagine her as a murderer. It didn't work.

As I worked my way through my ice cream, it seemed a good time to broach the subject of her continuing care. I am not the most finessed person on the planet, so I just laid it out there. "What are your plans for after I've gone home?" I said.

Startled, Lila seemed at a loss for words. "Well, I don't know," she said after a minute. Her eyes began to fill with tears and she rummaged for a tissue in her handbag. "I guess I've been dealing with James's death and I just haven't thought of it."

"I don't want to pressure you. Just to remind you that this is a very temporary arrangement so that you can be safe and have what you need until other, more permanent arrangements can be made."

"Well…." She seemed confused. "Well, yes, that's what we agreed. The trouble is, I don't *know* what I'll do after you're gone. I can't seem to get that far."

"Have you had a family meeting? Talked to the girls? They might have some ideas or be able to step up."

Lila pressed her lips to a napkin. She seemed uncomfortable. "Uh...no. Actually, I haven't talked with them about this yet."

She was not making this easier. "So maybe that would be the place to start," I said. "With a family meeting, something along those lines."

Lila's shoulders sagged and she again dabbed her eyes with the tissue. Then she stared out the window past the front of the car. "We're not so good at family meetings," she said.

I took in a mouthful of the ice cream cone. What's a person supposed to say to something like that? I just sat there and waited.

Finally Lila said, "I have a rather difficult relationship with my daughters."

I was taken aback. "All of them?" I said.

"I'm afraid so," she said. "It's a little better with Stephanie, but it's complicated."

I had all the time in the world. Plus, I'd made up my mind that by the end of the day we'd be in a real conversation about my exit plan. "Enlighten me," I said. "Oh, that sounded cold. I didn't mean it that way."

Lila wrapped the remainder of her ice cream cone in paper napkins and stuffed it in the tidy little trash receptacle on the floor between us. "Regan and Morgan have been out of my—our—lives for the past five years. I don't want to go into it, but that's the way it is. Stephanie always was very close to her father, and from a very young age wanted nothing more than to follow in his footsteps. She's protective. I know she loves me.

"She's very involved with winemaking and running the winery, but she has little real use for other people. She's so good at what she does, I don't think she could do anything else. She wouldn't want to. She works hard, she's a good person, but she's also weird. She is not the daughter for one to have a lovely mother-daughter relationship with. She's distant and prickly and difficult. She lives nearby, but we don't see each other that often."

Wow. That pretty much killed off the playing field. "Do you have any other options for family support?" I said.

Lila sighed. "Not really. I have two brothers in Iowa. We used to visit them when the girls were small, but neither of them has ever come to Oregon. At this stage I wouldn't want them to. Nobody from what's left of James's family even came to his memorial. He broke with them when he came to Oregon to start a vineyard rather than take over the family business."

Thank goodness for small families, I thought, after hearing about Lila's and James's. The idea of a deep family rift was distressing, even though it wasn't my family rift. The only person I had in the way of family was my daughter Darby, and she was on the East Coast. I started up the car and we rolled back toward the Dundee

Hills. This was not great news. Not that I had to solve the problem this minute, but it would be nice to return home a week from now, or less, knowing Lila was in good hands. Finally, I had a thought. "What about Lucila?"

"Lucila is a treasure. She also has a family with three small children who need her. She can't be with me at night."

Crap. "Does she have a relative who might be able to help you out at night?"

Lila thought about it for a minute, then nodded. "That's a really good idea," she said. "Better than any I've had so far. Lucila has cousins by the dozens."

Back at the estate, Lila headed for her room. Lucila was there, I could hear the vacuum running down the hall. That faint but unpleasant aroma still hung in the air like an unwanted guest. I checked the garbage before rummaging in the kitchen for lunch. Nothing seemed amiss there or in the fridge. I'd just taken out the remaining chicken salad and was scooping out a couple more of those large, ripe tomatoes when someone walked into the living room. It was Regan, oldest of the daughters.

She was dressed in a power suit, and she marched into the kitchen like she owned the place. "Where's Mom?" she said.

"Well, hello Regan," I said. "She was in her bedroom a moment ago."

Regan turned so quickly she slipped and nearly went down. Hah, I thought. That's what you get for prancing around in four-inch heels! She recovered quickly and marched in the direction of Lila's room.

I returned to my lunch preparation. "Cheeky cow," I muttered under my breath. Florian would be proud.

It looked as if we were in for family drama of some sort, because no sooner had she disappeared than Morgan popped her head around the bend into the kitchen. "Mom, is that you?" she asked. She was still wearing her sunglasses.

"No," I said. "She is in the bedroom with Regan."

"Oh, sorry," Morgan said. She wiggled her fingers at me and then disappeared into the vast bedroom, closing the door behind her.

I wiped my hands on a towel, and made my way toward the bedroom. Behind the closed door, voices were raised. I banged on the door with my fist before opening it. The three women stood, eyeing each other. Regan appeared hostile; Morgan had put on her best lost girl look; Lila, who clearly was exhausted, turned to face me. "Luncheon is served," I said, and she made a beeline for the door.

The girls followed close on her heels. I made Lila comfortable at the table and placed a stuffed tomato and buttered toast in front of her. I set my own lunch on the table and went back into the kitchen to retrieve the drinks and medications. Regan and Morgan pulled up chairs and sat down at the table across from Lila. "Can I get you ladies anything?" I asked as I seated myself at the end of the table.

"Do you have anything vegan?" Morgan said. Regan gave her a dirty look.

Hell no, I thought. "'fraid not," I said, and tucked into my chicken salad.

Regan, clearly in charge—she's the lawyer, after all—huffed and puffed a little and then said, "Mom, we've come to talk business. Can we get her out of here?" By "her", I assume she meant me. I looked at her and then turned to Lila for direction.

"You did not call ahead, and you have interrupted our lunch," Lila said. "So, no. Emma stays here. She can certainly hear whatever it is you have to say to me."

That went over like a fart in church, but things are what they are. The sisters looked at each other nonplussed. I took another bite of my salad, and then a sip of water.

"This is family business," Regan said.

Morgan the vegan chimed in. "Yes, and it's, like, *private*." She talked like a six-year-old, which probably came from talking to small children all the time.

Lila set her fork down and looked both of them over. Her expression remained neutral, passive even, and I, for one, couldn't imagine how she did it. "Emma is here staying with me, and has assumed the duties of a family member. Anything you have to say can be said in front of her."

Part of me felt like running away, but this was too good to miss. I stayed silent and very still, as if bolted to my chair.

"Very well, then," said Regan. "Mother, your health is frail at best. We're concerned about you, and the winery is just too much for you to worry about. Morgan and I have talked a lot about what's the best scenario here, and selling the winery would really take a big load off your shoulders. I realize Dad was angry when I brought up me and Morgan getting more involved five years ago at Christmas. I know we stepped on some toes, and I apologize. But it seems like the time is finally right for us to step in now and help you. I am happy to do all the legal work free of charge, and Morgan has an announcement to make."

Regan talked like she was addressing an audience where her advice had been solicited. To my knowledge, this was not the case. She was cool, confident, and laid the cards on the table. I glanced at Lila, who had turned a ghastly shade of white. An hour ago, in the car eating ice cream, she'd looked like a normal person out for a day of fun. This changed everything.

Before she could open her mouth, a very flushed Morgan chimed in, again talking in her primary school voice. "Mom, I know you are going to be so excited for me! I passed my real estate exam last week and I've been hired at one of the big firms in Portland. I can even handle all of the sales details for you. We can all work together as a family. It will be so much fun."

She stopped yammering. Lila said nothing. Sounds of deadly silence roared in my ears.

Lila gave it a couple minutes. I had to hand it to her for timing. It was all any of us could do to endure her silence. Finally she spoke. "Thank you for coming out today girls, and for thinking of me. I am not going to consider your proposal, although I appreciate the time you've put into it. There is no way I'd consider selling the winery. In the first place, it is absolutely no trouble to me. Stephanie—whom, I notice, is not at this meeting—is doing a fine job of running the winemaking aspects of the operation, and we have good people in place for sales, marketing, and vineyard management. I will have no trouble meeting with key people as the need arises and we have to make changes."

The sisters exchanged a look. Morgan said, "But mom—" Regan laid a hand on her arm to shut her up.

Then Lila cut in before Regan could say anything. "I wonder if either of you have considered that this is Stephanie's job, her livelihood, and her passion you are talking about here behind her back, not to mention my own" she said. "She would be utterly devastated if she knew you were here without her, hoping to get me to sell the winery out from under her. And, in fact, I cannot imagine how you managed to come up with such a callous proposal. Your dad is barely cold. I am on an aggressive treatment plan and am doing just fine heath-wise, thank you very much. And this is the first time in five years you've come up here to say anything to me or your father about the winery, or anything else important in our lives. I'm only grateful I still see the grandchildren from time to time.

"The winery's sales are up eighteen percent last fiscal year—this, despite all the new vineyards and wineries in the valley. This makes your claim even more preposterous. This winery provided all three of you with post-graduate educations so that you could pursue your dreams. I suggest you get back to them and rid yourselves immediately of any thoughts about what's best for me." She stood up from the table and made a little waving motion toward the door. "You both can leave now." Then she walked into her bedroom, closing the door quietly behind her.

Well, well.

Both Regan and Morgan flushed purple. They looked at each other, mouths open. Far from chastened, they were outraged. They seemed to have forgotten I was there.

"How can she think she's still in charge after all that's happened?" said Morgan.

Regan's nostrils flared as she looked toward the closed bedroom door. "She's clearly not in touch with reality. All that chemo has affected her brain. She's got to figure it out, and I am certain she will soon, that she can't keep doing this—not without Daddy, and certainly not as sick as she is."

Morgan pouted. "We can't wait forever," she said. "I need help now."

Regan turned her head quickly in my direction, as if suddenly remembering that I still sat at the table soaking up every word. She glared at me, eyes cold and dark as slate. "You're going to forget you ever heard this conversation," she said. "This is private family business, and it goes nowhere. I can't figure out why you're here anyway."

"Probably because your mother needs help and you aren't willing to provide it," I said. "No worries. We're having a great time together." So get lost, I thought. After this little scene, it was apparent that Lila wouldn't be safe with these two around. They'd be after her about selling the place, and it's doubtful they cared enough to attend to her needs. I didn't say another word to either of them, just sat there and watched. Enough already had been said.

Morgan rummaged in her designer handbag. Tears ran down her mottled red face. Regan looked her over and said, "Get a grip, Morgan." Then she rose from the table and dusted some nonexistent crumbs from her big-shot city lawyer suit, picked up her oversized satchel, and walked toward the door. The still teary Morgan bounced up and grabbed the handbag and sun glasses. She looked over her shoulder at me as she trotted out the door behind her big sister.

CHAPTER 13

I'm sure the Ryders kept booze in the house. At that moment it's a good thing I didn't know where it was. Maybe this is how pole vaulters feel. You start on *terra firma*, fly through the air, and end up in Camp WTF. It seems to have happened that quickly, and I was reeling. I couldn't even imagine what Lila was feeling at this moment? Abandoned? Betrayed? Those words and others would be high on my list.

It was obvious to me that the two older sisters needed money. Otherwise, why would they care about selling the winery? Why on earth would Regan need it? She was a member of the MAC. She could probably sell her membership for more than it was worth—if the esteemed members of the club allowed such things. Morgan, on the other hand, had a much lower income base than Regan, and was divorced with small children.

Lucila worked her way into the living room. I greeted her, then I finished my tomato and headed to Lila's inner sanctum. I rapped gently on her door.

"Come in."

It was dark in her bedroom. Shades up, curtains drawn. She sat on top of her bed, a grim expression on her face. "It's time to come out now," I said. "Coast is clear, and you still need your lunch."

"I'm not hungry."

"I don't expect you to be. So humor me. You need protein, and it's pill time, so let's get something in your system before you take them."

Lila heaved a sigh. "Goddammit! Just goddammit and hell and shit. I am so sick of this." She started to cry. "How could we have raised such creatures?" she blubbered into her hands.

I walked into the room and sat on the bed next to her. I put a tentative arm around her. "If they were mine, I'd be crying too," I said.

She shook beneath my arm, halfway between a laugh and a cry. "They're just despicable human beings. I don't understand how that happened. Five years ago at Christmas they came out here and offered for James and me to hand over control of the winery to them. He came unglued, of course. I can't even repeat some of the things he said. They haven't been back since. And now they're here with their hands out wanting to 'help' me? Good God!"

I patted her on the back. "Come on, old girl. You need some food." I got up and left the room. In a couple minutes, Lila came into the dining area and sat down. She'd washed her face, combed her hair, and put on lipstick. Even with reddened eyes, the overall effect was better than I expected. She took her pills and nibbled on a piece of toast, then ate about half of the stuffed tomato. Good job! I gave myself a pat on the back, too. She'd consumed nearly enough calories, if one counted the ice cream, to avert malnourishment.

It was nearing one, and I had the itch to get out of the house. "What do you have going this afternoon?" I said.

Lila pushed back her chair. "I'm going to bed. I'm going to cry, and then I'll read a mystery until I go to sleep. I feel like hell, and I just need to be alone."

Then came the inevitable question. "What do you want for dinner?" I said.

"Nothing."

"Aw, come on. We're better than this. How about a big, juicy cheeseburger?"

Lila lit up a bit. "That sounds like a really good idea. I almost think I could do that."

All right, then. I dusted my hands together. "Great. I'm going over to the Westerly for a swim, then I'll run a couple of errands and be home by six with cheeseburgers. Is there anything you need while I'm out?"

Lila grabbed a piece of paper and scribbled out a short list and handed it to me. "Don't worry about me," she said. "If I need anything, Lucila will be here until four." She then repaired to her bedroom. I trotted back to my room, where I stuffed my swimsuit, a towel, and sunscreen into a small tote. Freedom! I hopped in my car and got out of there before anything could change that.

It was a lazy summer afternoon at the Westerly. Angel was just finishing her lunch when I showed up in the kitchen. She jumped to her feet and hugged me. "Oh, Senora, I am so glad to see you. Please, sit. I have cookies."

The magic word. I plopped, and a plate of round, buttery, lemony, crunchy cookies appeared before me. I'd downed about four of them before I remembered why I had come to visit in the first place. "Oh, Angel," I said. "These are heavenly, but I came to swim. I can't sit here eating, because after the swim I must return to Lila Ryder's house to fix her dinner."

Angel, who'd been bustling around me, picked up the plate. "I understand, Senora. I will prepare you a package. You can take the cookies to Senora Ryder."

She whisked the cookies away. I whisked myself into the downstairs powder room and changed into my swimsuit. "Where's Melody today?" I asked Angel on my way out the door.

"She is in Portland, Senora. She has the business to do today. The errands."

Good. I'd have a peaceful swim and catch up with her later. Out at the pool, I spread my towel on a lounge chair and dived into the water. The pool always was kept at a pleasant temperature, but our little heat wave had upped the water's warmth by several degrees. I swam several laps, floated around a bit, and even did a few exercises in the shallow water. For some reason I had the place to myself, and it was heavenly.

All the guests were doing other things. Even the gardeners had gone home. Without any distractions, I was able to let my mind wander freely over the past several days' events. As I played in the water, I thought about James's memorial and the thugs. Kudos to Florian for setting them straight. There was the chef's knife, which managed to bug me a lot—possibly because I very well could be staying with the wielder of the knife. And then my brain settled on the curious situation of Max Weatherman and his wrecked car up on Bald Peak. Had it been stolen? And, once again, where the hell was he anyway? Everyone in the county wanted to speak with him, and he hadn't actually been seen since the day after the salmon bake. It made no sense.

Then there were those daughters. Their arrival, the brusqueness, the rudeness they had shown to Lila in front of me was nothing less than alarming. Who were they to barge into her house and tell her, a perfectly capable woman, what to do? It worried me for her.

Morgan's childish desperation showed, but Regan was just downright conniving and nasty. What was the payoff for Regan if Lila were to sell the winery? Did she need money too, or was she just flexing her fat-cat attorney muscles to help her sister? It was a puzzle, and a very disturbing one at that.

My thoughts were interrupted by the honking of a car horn. I looked toward the house to see Melody standing by her Mini Cooper blasting away. I waved. She waved. Then she trotted across the lawn to the pool. "Come on in and have some tea," she called from the fence surrounding the pool area. "We can talk."

I wasn't ready yet. "I need a few more minutes, Mel. I'll be with you in a bit." Melody turned back to the house, and I climbed out of the pool. I toweled off, greased myself generously with sunscreen, and lay back on the lounge chair. The sunshine warmed me, but my thought processes had been interrupted. I closed my eyes to enjoy the warmth

Suddenly I jerked awake. What time was it? I pulled my watch out of the tote bag. I'd probably dozed for half an hour. I looked at my expanses of white meat. They hadn't yet turned red—a good thing. I got up, ran a comb through my hair, folded my towel, and headed for the house. While I'd dozed, company had come to the Westerly in the form of a big black sedan.

I walked onto the deck and tried to open the slider. It was locked. Melody sat at the table with a couple of men in suits. She mouthed, "Go around!" and waved me away. Curiouser and curiouser. I shrugged and walked around the house to the front door. Thankfully, it was unlocked. I changed in the powder room, returned to my car, and put my swim gear in the trunk. I peeked onto the deck and the three of them were still at it in the kitchen. With few options, I got in my car and drove down to Newberg to run Lila's errands.

I was browsing amid the lettuces when my cell phone rang. Melody. "You've got to come back," she said the moment I answered. "I have so *much* to tell you!"

"Yes," I said. "Who were those men?"

"I'll tell you when you get here." She hung up.

Oh, God, what now? I wondered. I bagged up some lettuce, and grabbed a few more vegetables plus the items on Lila's list. Then I made my way back to the Westerly as quickly as was possible in the afternoon traffic.

When I arrived, Melody was on the front porch holding court with her guests while they ate hazelnuts and little cheesy bits and drank local wine. It was the familiar ritual I'd observed every day from four to five in the afternoon when I'd stayed here the previous autumn. When she spotted me driving toward the house, she stood up and excused herself. She was waiting for me on the deck when I pulled up in back.

"Thank goodness you're here," she said, and ushered me into the kitchen. Angel had gone home for the day, so we had the place to ourselves, except for Winston. Her eyes were large, and she nearly danced with excitement. "Those guys were FBI agents. You remember those nice men from last March in Bandon? They're the same ones, and they want me to help them catch the thugs!"

I thought those guys looked familiar. I didn't even want to think about them, and I don't remember them as being particularly nice. I certainly couldn't imagine how my friend was going to help them. "You said no, of course," I said.

"Absolutely not. I told them I'd be happy to help in any way I can." She looked so pleased with herself, while I, the sensible one, knew this only could lead to misery for someone. "They have the best plan, and since the Carriage House isn't rented until the middle of next week, it'll just be perfect."

I'd heard those words before. It inevitably turned into something akin to "I Love Lucy" on crack. When I could bring myself to speak, I said, "What's the plan?"

Melody clasped her hands together. "Well. You *know* Max's wife is in town. And *they* want to put her up in the Carriage House.

They'll pay, of course. And they figure the thugs will come after her, hoping that she will lead them to Max. How smart is that?"

"Oh, it's just great, as long as you and your guests aren't caught in the middle of a shootout. I mean Jesus, Melody, if that happened it would ruin you."

"Why are you always such a wet blanket?"

"Listen, we've both been in a situation where people got killed. It wasn't that long ago. Remember?" Unfortunately, that was one of the things that could and did still keep me awake at night. "Why do the FBI want to catch the thugs anyway?"

Melody quickly filled me in. Weatherman's business partner in WeatherVane had drowned in his bathtub three weeks previous. While there was no proof that the man hadn't died naturally, given his blood alcohol level and the drugs in his system, suspicion surrounded the death. In fact, the same people who were investigating WeatherVane's activities had also begun investigating the business partner's untimely demise. Supposedly Weatherman had left town because he was concerned for his own safety.

Weatherman and his partner had been engaged in what the FBI told Melody were "questionable practices" regarding the management of their properties, and possible ties to unsavory "connected" people—so much so that their business, which was active in several western states, had been monitored by the Feds for the past several months.

"One of the agents told me they think Max's partner was pushed under the water," Melody said, barely able to control her excitement. "So Weatherman's wife is more than happy to be in Oregon too. She's afraid they might come after her next to get even with Weatherman, since he has been seriously cheating the wrong people."

I asked her who the "wrong people" might be.

"Why, the mob, of course," Melody said. "Those guys pissed off the mob. So they killed the partner. At least that's what the agents think. And now those awful men are up here looking for Weatherman so they can get even with him, too. Why, just six weeks ago, they beat the crap out of him and left him unconscious near the gate of one of his fancy real estate developments."

God help us. She'd lost her mind and really was going to go through with this. "Melody, why are you getting yourself involved with this? Somebody could get hurt. Let them do this somewhere else."

"I feel sorry for the wife," she said. "Marla—that's her name—is staying in Portland at Max's condo, and they want her to come out here tomorrow. By herself, of course. And check in. And they'll just take it from there. One or both of them will stay out there with her. There are two beds. And then, when those guys come after her they'll nab 'em."

Just shoot me now, I thought. "Groovy." The word dripped sarcasm. "I hope I'm back in Portland when the shit hits the fan. And why didn't they do this at the condo instead of out here? You will regret this, you know. Those FBI guys don't think of anybody or anything but their cases and themselves. So, if you or somebody else gets hit in the cross-fire, it'll be just tough shit and so be it."

Melody just shrugged, but I could tell she was angry with me. "I knew you'd be this way. How else are they supposed to catch criminals? Heck, maybe Max will show up himself, and that mystery will be solved. I feel it's my duty as a citizen to help. Here I thought you'd be pleased for me."

That was a good one. I let it pass. "You know his car has been found."

"Yes, I saw it on the news last night."

"Nobody in it. No blood. No sign of him. I'm betting they already got to him and he's dead. Those goon types play for keeps."

Still, Melody plowed forward undeterred. "Well, you just think what you want," she said. "I'm meeting Marla tomorrow and will find out all I can. And I'll finally get Max's shit out of my basement."

I'd had enough. "I gotta go," I said. "Lila awaits."

Melody walked to the refrigerator, pulled out a large metal pan, and set it in a shopping bag on the counter. "Dan's first shipment of fish came yesterday," she said. "Flash-frozen halibut and salmon. Angel was beside herself, as I knew she would be, and she whipped up some halibut enchiladas with tomatillo sauce. She wanted you and Lila to have some. And also a bunch of her cookies." She turned and presented me with the bag. "This should keep you going for a couple of days."

I hugged her and took the bag. "Yeah, well, that's super. Thanks Melody. Break a leg. I hope nobody gets killed. Dan needs to take you on another vacation when he gets back, just to keep you out of trouble."

She walked me to the door and blew a kiss as I walked out to the car. "I'll let you know what happens."

I bet you will, I thought. But I was looking forward to a really good dinner. The cheeseburgers would have to wait.

Thank God for uneventful evenings. Lila went crazy for the halibut enchiladas, even though she was unable to eat much. I ate more than my share, and we still had enough left for the next day and then some. After dinner, we sat on the deck, drank our decaf, and ate Angel's delicious cookies. We chit-chatted for an hour, and I felt myself growing close to this woman I'd known only peripherally for the past twenty-eight years. It's a shame that James had been such a showboat. And when I had my journalist hat on, he often was the one who had the information I needed to meet the next deadline. Under different circumstances, I would have made the opportunity to know her much better.

About eight-thirty, Lila stood up. "I'm going to bed," she said. "I'm going to take my pills and read something really raunchy to get my mind off those daughters of mine until I fall asleep."

I jumped to my feet and walked into the house with her. I watched her take her medications because I am such a great nurse and that's how we did it in rehab. Make sure every one of those suckers goes down. Then if something happens, one can be very certain what to tell the docs about medications. Better to be safe, and all that.

Then I locked up the house and moseyed down the hall to my room. I was beat, but not too beat to write all about the day's happenings in my journal. I possibly would need this information in the future. And it's better to be safe….

CHAPTER 14

Next morning, as Dawn's rosy fingers crept over the eastern hills, I made a pot of strong coffee. I'd slept well, showered, and was ready to kick butt. It was only six-thirty, but when one goes to bed with the chickens one is ready to get up with them.

Standing on the deck, sipping my coffee, I remembered it was Cat's birthday. How could we best celebrate? Especially with me out here every night? Suddenly, something or some*one* moved in the vineyard. Probably it was just the deer out for a morning browse, but for some reason the movement struck me as furtive. Something didn't feel right.

I donned my running shoes and headed down the deck stairs and into the area between two rows of vines to have a look. Slowly, quietly, I walked about thirty yards into the vineyard without seeing anything but grapevines. I paused to listen, and decided to turn back, when something rustled behind me. I began to turn around, and was grabbed from behind. I opened my mouth to scream, and strange hand clapped over it. Terrified, I twisted sharply and we landed on the ground with a painful thunk.

Pained grunt. It was a man, and he was beneath me so he'd gotten the worst of it. Frenzied, I twisted my body again in an attempt to get away, but he just hung on tighter. I tried to elbow him in the gut, but he had too tight a grip on my arms. However, I got really lucky when I dropped my head forward, then swung it back as hard as I could. I felt my skull connect with his nose. There was a gristly crunch.

He sounded like a girl when he squealed out in pain, but he let go of me for an instant. And then he yelled some choice words, mostly having to do with female anatomy. Before I could escape he grabbed ahold of me again, and this time he tried to strangle me. I flipped my body again and we rolled in the dirt, kicking and scratching. His forearm brushed my face and I bit it. Hard. He screamed again, and yanked out a handful of my hair. I roared in pain.

"Stop!" A man's voice pierced the mayhem. Someone stood above us looking down. I took a quick glance at him and continued writhing and kicking. It was the weasel! Oh shit! I was dead!

"Settle down, sister. Nobody's gonna hurt ya." The weasel had a Jersey Shore accent. I also noticed that he had a gun in his hand. Although it wasn't aimed at me, I stopped struggling. "Let 'er go, Pete. We gotta talk." He'd lost the Hawaiian shirt and was wearing jeans, a tight black t-shirt, and running shoes.

Pete, a bit the worse for wear I hoped, took his sweaty mitts off me. Groaning, I crawled to my knees and then struggled to my feet. Completely freaked out, I started in on the weasel. "What the hell are you doing here? And why is this guy trying to kill me? I never did anything to you! And besides, you're trespassing. Don't you know you could be bringing disease into—?"

"Shaddup!"

He had the upper hand—I mean, with two of them and a firearm, of course he did—but I still was madder than a nest of scalded wasps for being rolled around in the dirt and choked. Not to mention the loss of hair and being scared out of my mind. "Ex-*cuse* me?" I sounded pretty tough, even to me.

"I'm Marv." The weasel switched the gun to his left hand and stuck out his right hand.

"I'm not going to shake hands with you, and I don't give a shit who you are," I said. I put my hands behind my back. Hopefully they wouldn't kill me because of a spurned handshake. "Now, if you wouldn't mind telling me what you're doing here and why you beat up on me." The least they could do was apologize.

"And we don't like strangers wandering around in our vineyards, either," I said. "Because we never know where else they've been and what they might have on their shoes." To my knowledge, the Ryder Estate vines were still on their original rootstock, and with phylloxera, a prolific root louse that was running rampant in the Willamette Valley, not to mention other assorted pests, one could never be too careful.

Marv held up his hands for silence. "Lady, will ya please just shut up. This is Pete. Like I said, if ya shut up and settle down, we won't hurt ya." When he said "hurt" it came out "hoit".

Pete scrambled to his feet. He re-tied his shoes and dusted himself off. He too wore blue jeans and a black t-shirt—perfect for sneaking around on someone else's property. I noticed a small trickle of blood from his left nostril, and my bite had broken the skin on his arm. He glared at me. "You better get that looked at," I said, nodding to his wounded arm. "I haven't had my shots."

Both men were medium height, fit, and looked to be in their early forties. But my God, here I was in the middle of a vineyard with a couple of Las Vegas murderers. What was the world coming to? I truly *was* living in Camp WTF, and it had to stop.

Marv ignored my remark about trespassers. "We're looking for a friend," he said.

"Who might that be, and why would he be anywhere near here at six-thirty in the morning?" I said.

"His name is Max Weatherman."

"I know who he is, and I can't help you," I said. "I last saw him the Sunday morning after the IPNC Salmon Bake, and that was more than a week ago."

"Yeah, but we think he was around here just the other day," Marv said.

"Well, think what you like. Nobody's seen him in more than a week?"

"They found his BMW on Tuesday."

"I know that. So what? That's just the car. He wasn't in it."

"How do you know?"

I shrugged and quoted my friend Rob the Reporter. "No body, no blood, no nothing."

The two men looked at each other. "Nah," said Pete. "Not possible."

"How do you know?" the weasel—I mean Marv—said again.

"Listen, I think you're wasting your time here," I said. "I'm telling you everything I know. I have a friend who gives me inside information from the local police departments, and Max Weatherman was not in that car when it crashed or there would have been some sort of evidence in and around the vehicle. It was clean. They think the car may have been stolen and then rolled down that hillside. As for your Max Weatherman, he probably went back to Nevada a week ago and you just aren't in the loop"

"He ain't there," said Marv. "The boss told us to keep looking."

"Well," I informed him, "other people—sheriffs, police, what-have-you, are looking for him too. His wife even came up here. Just in case you didn't know. If they can't find him, how do you think you're going to do it? Do you have a helicopter we all don't know about? And what do you want with him anyway?"

"None-a-ya business, sister."

Pete piped in. "We come up here 'cuz the boss wants him to come back to Vegas with us. We ain't gonna hurt 'im."

I just bet they weren't going to hoit him. For my money, Max already had been hoit. "Sorry I can't help you. You might want to talk to Marla. I understand she's staying at the Westerly while she's up here."

New information, at least for them. A look passed between them, and then Marv said, "Yeah, well, thanks for the tip."

"Sure. Can I go now?"

"Yeah, catch ya later." They both saluted me with two fingers, then took off down the hill.

I was safe, at least for the moment, and I could quit pretending I wasn't scared senseless. I walked with as much dignity as possible up the hill, which, considering the state of my bladder, wasn't much. It was only by the grace of God that I hadn't peed my pants.

I entered the house through the slider. Lila was in the kitchen pouring herself a cup of coffee. Her mouth dropped open when she saw me. "Oh my word! What on earth happened to you?" she said.

"Oh, you won't believe it," I said, and streaked down the hall to the bathroom. It took me a few minutes to collect myself.

When I returned she was seated at the counter waiting for me. I grabbed myself a mug and filled it with coffee. Then I sat down next to her.

"You're filthy!" she said. "What were you doing out there so early?" she asked. "Did you fall?"

I took a big gulp of coffee. "As a matter of fact I did," I said. "With help." I told her about the trespassers and my little roll in the dirt.

"That's horrible," she said. "I'm going to call the police. It's a good thing they didn't run into Stephanie. She would have straightened them out—most likely with James's twenty-two. That could have been bad."

I thought of their aggressive behavior when they visited Melody. "We'll call them. They need to be told about this," I said. "Hopefully they'll be able to find these guys before they attack someone else."

Lila took a sip of coffee. She looked me up and down again and said, "Do you need to go to Emergency?" There were no visible signs of concern about strangers roaming around her property uninvited.

I felt the newly bald patch on the side of my head. Other than that, it was mostly just a few scratches and bruises. "I'm not really hurt," I said. "Just shook up. I was lucky, and I'll be fine. I think a phone call will suffice."

I thought about my encounter for about moment. "I think they just wanted information," I said. "They really only want Weatherman. But I don't like the idea of you being up here alone. Don't you think you might want to look into getting a big, noisy dog?"

"If somebody wanted to get us they would have done it by now," Lila said. "But don't worry, we have a state-of-the-art alarm system. And in my condition, I'm not going to be out wandering in the vineyard."

"You don't seem worried."

"I'm not worried. Unless they do something destructive, which doesn't seem likely. Hopefully they'll just move on. When you've had breast cancer twice and your husband has just been murdered it rather puts things in perspective, don't you think? I am more concerned about getting through this day than I am with a couple of stupid men."

That explained a lot. How stupid the thugs were remained to be seen. But if they went to the Westerly looking for Marla, they would walk into the welcoming arms of two FBI agents, and that would be the end of their skulking around on other people's property beating up on older women. I told Lila as much, and she laughed.

"And speaking of cancer," Lila said, "I have my chemo tomorrow at one. I'm not able to drive, so I hope you are available."

Of course I was available. "That's why I'm here," I said. Then I thought once again of Cat's birthday. "I do have a little issue today, however," I told her, and explained the situation. "I'd could go into Portland and make her dinner. But if you don't mind, I'd rather invite her out here and cook for all of us."

Lila perked up. "That would be a treat for me," she said. "Maybe, if it wouldn't be too much trouble, you could invite Melody too? I'd love to spend some time with her."

The best of all worlds! "Thanks, Lila. Now I just have to put it together." My brain started running on a menu and how to pull off a dinner party for five at the last minute. Maybe we could have waited a couple of days, but I wanted to get it done that night in case Lila had a bad reaction to her chemo and wouldn't feel like eating.

I made breakfast. After we ate, I took my second shower of the day, and then it was Lila's turn. While she was in her shower, I got on the phone. First I talked to Detective Haymore. He was more than a little interested in my adventure with the thugs. "Why didn't you keep them there?" he said. "We need to talk to those guys."

Keep them? Hell, I was glad to get rid of them. "That's your department," I said. "Be watching for them over at the Westerly. I told them Marla Weatherman is hanging out there."

That got his attention as I'm not sure he even knew about the FBI set-up. "Will do, and thanks for the tip," he said. "Do you need to go to Emergency or anything?"

I thought you'd never ask. "No, I'm okay. And I don't want you coming over here to look at me. Call me if you need anything else." I hung up.

Then I called Cat and wished her a happy birthday. She confirmed her availability for the dinner instantly, and told me Florian would be attending with her. Hmmm. Romance definitely had bloomed in Lower Hillsdale Heights.

Finally, I dialed Melody's number. "Dinner tonight at Lila's," I said when she picked up. It's Cat's birthday and we're having a party. And Florian's coming too."

"That old tomcat," said Melody. "He hasn't been here the last two nights. Stops by to change clothes and pinch Angel's bottom, and that's about it."

Aha. My suspicions confirmed. "Well, I'm just thrilled for Cat," I said. "I only hope she doesn't take it too hard when he returns to New York."

"I could be wrong, but I think he's pretty smitten. He said he's staying another week, but he didn't ask to stay here. Which is a good thing, because I'm booked." Goodness. It sounded like all-out love.

Lila emerged from the bathroom wrapped in a summer robe. "I am so excited about our dinner," she said. "Now that I'm safely out of the shower, you may be excused. I imagine you have a lot of work to do to get ready for tonight. I'll pick out some wines from the cellar."

"I'm starting with a major shopping trip," I said. "Do you need anything?"

She jotted down her usual few items, and I was on my way, planning as I slogged through the Dundee traffic to the Newberg Fred Meyer. I found most of what I wanted there, and stopped at a fruit stand on my way back to the house. The peaches were ripe and aromatic, and a peach galette seemed like just the ticket for a birthday treat.

Back at the estate, I unloaded the groceries. Lila was in her bedroom with the door closed. I peeked in on her, and she was asleep. With more than an hour before I needed to start preparing lunch, I mixed up some piecrust pastry, wrapped it, and set it to chill in the refrigerator. Then I put on some lipstick and set out on foot to the winery, where I hoped to have a little heart-to-heart with Stephanie and see where she stood on family matters.

I found her in the barrel room moving hoses. She wore Carhartt shorts and a grungy looking Nirvana t-shirt, topped with a leather apron. Her greasy hair was pulled back into a ponytail. I called her name and she looked up at me, then dropped the hoses and stood with her hands on her hips as I approached her.

I reached out my hand and said, "Hi Stephanie, I'm Emma. I'm staying with your mom until we can set up something more permanent."

She eyed me as if I might have something contagious, and then reluctantly extended her hand. "Hi," she said. "Yeah, I know who you are. What do you want?"

I cut to the chase. "I need to talk to you about your mom," I said. "I'm staying with her for a few days because she is too sick to be alone. She needs someone to make certain she eats, takes her medications, and doesn't fall in the shower, things like that."

The look Stephanie gave me told me nothing. "Let's go into my office," she said.

I followed her from the barrel room into the part of the winery that housed the tasting room and offices. Like everything else since my move to Portland, the winery was different—updated, more commercial. The former funky pioneering look had disappeared. There was a small gift shop offering mostly wine accessories such as monogram glasses, wine openers, and a few non-perishable snacks.

Stephanie escorted me into her office, sat down at her desk, and gestured me to a chair. "So, what do you think I'm supposed to do about this?" she asked after I'd sat down.

I shook my head. "I don't know. Ideally, you and your sisters would get involved and either find someone who works as a caregiver and is able to spend nights out here, or work out something among yourselves where you participate in her care in some way."

Stephanie didn't say anything. She just nodded. I plowed forward. "I wonder if you and your sisters have talked to each other about the situation and what needs to be done?"

"We haven't talked about it," she said. Her eyes were fixed on me without expression. "Regan said Mom's going to sell the winery."

Shocked by the revelation, I tried to choose my words carefully. "I very much doubt that," I told her. "When people are grieving like your mom is, they know it's not a good time to make decisions. I've been with her for a few days now, and she hasn't said anything to me about it. In fact, she's been telling me what a great job you do. Is it possible Regan may be mistaken?"

"She's sure about it," said Stephanie, "and I don't like it."

"Stephanie, your mom is a very fair person. If she were thinking about such a thing, which I very much doubt, she'd do the right thing. She'd get all of you girls together and talk about it with all of you before she made any plans. I can tell you most assuredly that you don't have to worry about that now."

Stephanie looked doubtful, but at least I think I made her question her sister's lies.

"Well, okay," she said. "Now, I don't want to talk about this anymore. My plate is full. If Mom needs help, she's smart enough to figure out what to do. I don't know anything about it and I have to get back to work."

That was that. Stephanie stood up, indicating it was time for me to go away. I'd made no progress, but I had learned another thing or two about the Ryder family dynamics. The news on that front wasn't good. And I was still stuck trying to help Lila figure things out without familial involvement.

CHAPTER 15

Our guests arrived promptly at seven in the Westerly Mercedes, a great big honkin' black sedan with tinted glass. It was Dan's car, but Melody couldn't cram more than one extra person into her Mini, especially when one of them was Florian's size. For someone taking her sixth turn at being 49, Cat looked stunning—all tan and long legs and the type of shit-eating grin you only get from good sex. Florian looked pretty pleased with himself, too. Melody was Melody.

Since the night was so fine, I'd set a table on the deck. We started with bruschetta topped with a choice of tapenades—olive and tomato-basil with fresh mozzarella. For the main course I made ahi tuna salads Nicoise. As the sun was setting, I presented the peach galette with a candle.

Cat blew out the candle and we wallowed in dessert as she opened her birthday gifts—including a very lovely diamond pendant from Florian. She looked happier than I'd ever seen her. Stars appeared—more stars than one will ever see in Portland after dark. Candles flickered and guttered on the table. We lingered in the balmy night, relaxing over coffee as we visited, laughed, and shared memories of those exciting early days in the Willamette Valley wine industry—stories I knew Florian would take home with him to use for reference and for future columns.

I felt content, lazy, a bit tired. It had been a long day of cooking, even if you didn't count my post-dawn adventure in the vineyard, shopping, and looking after Lila. I was about to excuse myself and head for bed when a substantial something hit the window behind and above us with a thwack, followed by a sharp cracking sound from the vineyard.

I'd heard that sound before. It was a rifle!

Florian acted the fastest. "Get down, get down!" he hissed. Without making a sound, we all hit the deck. Florian overturned chairs getting to Cat. He threw his body over hers. "Nobody move." He said it softly, and he meant business. We waited a couple minutes. Nothing. Then, without a word, he peeled himself off Cat and crawled toward the sliding glass doors. The inside lights went dark.

We lay on the deck in the silence. Even the crickets and night birds had gone silent after the gunshot. Florian returned to the deck, this time upright, and moved swiftly across it. Nothing happened. I noticed he carried something, and it looked like a pistol. My mind grappled with questions. Where did it come from? Does he normally carry a gun? No. It was crazy. I couldn't hear him tiptoe down the steps and into the vineyard, but I knew where he was going. For the second time in the same day I was scared out of my mind. But I kept quiet. We all kept quiet, because now he was out there alone and we didn't know what it meant.

We lay on the deck for what seemed like an eternity. Minute after minute crept by. It may have been half an hour. After a bit, the crickets tuned up and resumed their cheeping. I heard small animal rustlings beneath the deck. Once again the night birds called to each other, their normalcy restored.

I nearly dozed. And then, suddenly, Florian was back on the deck. I jerked wide awake. "All clear, ladies," he said. "The excitement is over for the evening. Where can I find some bloody Scotch?"

He walked inside and flipped on the lights. Then he got out his cell phone and dialed 9-1-1. We followed him in. Stiff from lying prone on the deck, Lila was having trouble walking. I moved close to her. "Go to bed," I said. "We'll take care of everything out here and I'll bring you your pills in a minute."

"But what about the police?" she said.

"If they need to talk to you, I know where to find you."

Gratefully she nodded, and said her goodnights. I busied myself with the window shades. If someone was still out there, at least he couldn't see us. Or they. Perhaps it was the thugs, come back for more excitement.

Florian located the booze and poured himself a stiff one. He held the bottle up. "Anybody else?" We shook our heads. And then he poked around until he found a large flashlight, which he beamed up to the ceiling and shined it all over until he found where the bullet had imbedded. "Look at that," he said, pointing to the spot. "For it to hit over here, the shooter would have been about fifty yards down the vineyard. Either he's a Luddite when it comes to firearms, or he had no intention of hurting us. Any opinions?"

I told him about my morning adventure with the goons. "Bloody hell, woman, why didn't you tell us earlier?"

"You could have been killed," said Melody.

"Yes, but I wasn't," I said. "I got rolled in the dirt and broke a guy's nose, but they really just wanted to find Max Weatherman. Or so they said. I'll be sore for a couple of days and the sheriff's department knows all about it."

Florian scooted his chair closer to Cat and put his arm around her. "I don't think anyone's going to find him any time soon," he said. "At least not alive." Cat shuddered and he squeezed her tighter.

"So it could have been the thugs again, but based on what they told me, I can't think why they'd come back. And if they didn't do it, who did?" I said.

Florian took a sip of his scotch. "Whoever killed Weatherman, darling."

"So you really think he's dead," I said.

"One hundred percent yes, I do. If his people don't know his whereabouts and nobody here can find him, you can be bloody certain something's happened to him."

I excused myself to take Lila her medications. Then I came back into the living room and sat with the others. The sheriff's deputies, including my friends Haymore and Jeffers, showed up about fifteen minutes later. We all went through the formalities and then Haymore sent his minions down into the vineyard with big lights. He, Jeffers, and Florian huddled on the deck.

When they came back in, Florian said, "We're going to look for evidence, ladies." And off they went.

"Well," said Melody, when the men had departed, "shall we get out the Port and cigars?"

I had to hand it to her. After being shot at, she was still in the game. But, to put it in perspective, we'd been through much worse. Since the window hadn't shattered and sliced us to bits, we were doing okay.

The men returned from their explorations about half an hour later. Florian saw the detectives to the door. They all but ignored us. When he was done seeing them out, he returned to the living room and made eye contact with Cat. "Time to go, darling. We have a long drive back to Portland."

She nodded. Then I piped in, "What about us? Aren't you going to tell us what happened?"

Florian looked my way. "It looks as if there may have been two people out there," he said. "The deputies are taking some casts for footprints, but it's hard to tell if they'll get anything conclusive. They did want me to tell 'Mrs. Ryder' that they'd be back in the morning to see what they can find when it's daylight."

"What about the bullet?"

Florian rubbed the top of his fuzzy scalp. "I expect they'll want that, too. You'd best warn Lila."

Sounded like we were in for another big day. "Did they say anything about my brush with the thugs?" I asked.

"No, darling. They didn't, but I'm sure it will take care of itself in the goodness of time."

With that, Florian, Cat, and Melody gathered their belongings and were gone. I went around the house and locked every door and window. Then I stepped out onto the deck for a brief peek. Lights glowed down in the vineyard, so the deputies were hard at work. Who knew how long they'd be there.

I locked the slider and was just headed to the kitchen to start cleaning up when Lila rolled out into the living room in her wheelchair. "I can't sleep," she said.

"What's up?"

"I can't stop thinking about James. What a ghastly way to die! Someone is after us, and tonight it could have been me."

"Why would anyone be after you," I said.

Lila rolled a little closer. I grabbed a chair from the dining room table, turned it around, and sat down. "I can't think of any reason other than that spa," she said. "People want access to that property and we're—I am—interfering with their plans."

I thought about it for a few seconds. "Yes, that's the way it seemed to me, too," I said. "But the zoning is up to the county, and if you don't like the county's decision, you can always hire a lawyer and make a real stink. With Weatherman out of action—at least that's the assumption—and the guys looking for him, who else is left? Do you have any ideas on that one?"

She signed. "I don't know. Something's bothering me, but I can't quite put a finger on it."

I stood up. "Well, you'd better get some rest. We have a big day tomorrow." I moved back into the kitchen and grabbed a carton of milk from the refrigerator. "Let me fix you one of Ma Golden's famous sleeping potions. It worked for me when I was a kid." I poured a mug full of milk and heated it in the microwave, then added a rounded spoonful of honey, stirred, and topped it with a quick grind of nutmeg. I did a quick taste test. Excellent, and its soporific benefits never ceased to amaze.

Mug in hand, I led the way back to Lila's bedroom. I helped her into bed and propped her up. I handed her the mug. "Here, and happy trails," I said. "You'll feel sleepy very soon." I left her all tucked in and returned to the kitchen to finish cleaning up.

Later, in my bedroom writing, something was nagging at me too. It had to do with the eight-inch chef's knife that originated in the Ryder kitchen and had severed James Ryder's aorta. Lila Ryder was a cool number. She'd had access to the knife, of course, but it seemed too obvious. The police thought so too, or they would have arrested her. Who else could have gotten their hands on the knife was anybody's guess. A whole winery full of people at work a hundred yards away, including one of the Ryder daughters.

Lila was more than a little relaxed about locking doors. And if she had been involved, what was her motive? She appeared to be in genuine shock, grieving her husband's death. In life she'd been his partner in work and on the home front. Provided she did, for some reason, want to get rid of James, it would take timing and planning and strength. She didn't have the strength, for starters. And surely she wouldn't be stupid enough to choose a murder weapon from her own knife drawer. It really made no sense to even go there. And what about that shot from the vineyard? Bad aim? That puzzled me too. Hopefully the sheriff's detectives would get to the bottom of it.

CHAPTER 16

Another day in Paradise. I woke up early, seized by a burning need to know what had happened down in the vineyard the night before. I started the coffee, took my shower, and was dressed and down amid the grapes, steaming mug of coffee in hand, just as the sun rose over the distant hills.

The vineyard was cool and crisp. Despite yesterday's dramas, I felt alone and safe. The ubiquitous crime scene tape surrounded a moderate-size patch of grapes. I walked the perimeter, peering in to see what was being protected. Yes, there were footprints. But how does one distinguish between the ones that belong there and those of someone who doesn't? Not only had the thugs and I been down there stirring stuff up not that long ago, but there also were several vineyard workers who walked up and down those rows all the time.

My explorations yielded nothing. Disappointed I returned to the house, which after time in the vineyard smelled worse than ever. I spent an hour drinking coffee and reading the newspaper. Lila emerged from her bedroom about seven-thirty. Then it was time to get going with breakfast, medications, and her shower. We were due at St. Vincent's Hospital at ten for her chemotherapy treatment.

Just before ten found me wheeling Lila into the hospital cancer center. I got her checked in and headed straight for my bungalow in Lower Hillsdale Heights. Once there, I opened things up to air out the place, then took up the hose and began watering. I read all my mail and paid a few bills. I was alone. Bliss. I could think and just chill out for a couple of hours.

There was no shortage of things to think about. In addition to the murder, disturbing things had happened out at the Ryder Estate vineyard. I was sore from being thumped around by those creeps yesterday. The gunshot last night indicated that someone could be after Lila. Where firearms were concerned, I never took things lightly. The shot was fired from Lila's vineyard and at Lila's house. Could it all come back to the spa? With James gone, perhaps the behavior was directed at scaring her into selling the place.

Motive, means, opportunity. The person with an obvious motive, something to gain from James's death and its fallout, Max Weatherman, had inconveniently disappeared. The guys from Las Vegas were no help. Sure they were looking for Weatherman, to do God knows what with him. But other than that, where did they fit in? Was it their job to scare us all to death and thus pave the way for WeatherVane's owners to come up and install that resort up the hill? Based on my meeting with them, those two were not the decision makers. If they did anything, it was someone else's behest.

That left us with not very much. Lila wasn't a credible suspect. I thought about the daughters, but only briefly. No doubt my two favorite detectives had a handle on things. But I still could be curious. And what about that Florian Craig? Wasn't he just tight as a tick with those two? What had he been doing with them out in the vineyard last night? More important, what was he doing alone in the vineyard, in the dark, with a *gun*? It occurred to me that he may have borrowed Melody's Glock. But why bring a gun to a dinner party? He sure as heck wasn't traveling with something like that in this post-9/11 day and age. Florian Craig, Man of Mystery. I'd been friends for years with a man I knew nothing about.

I glanced at my watch. It was time to pick up Lila and take her home to rest. I'd made the best of the situation to date, but if I'd wanted to be a nurse I would have gone to school and gotten my degree in nursing. It was a strain. I guess if nobody else was going to talk to those knucklehead daughters of hers, I'd have to do it. The other two, not Stephanie. She seemed to have enough problems just functioning on the planet. And if Regan and Morgan didn't step up, then Lila and I were going to have to make a plan. Quickly. I'd helped out, but I did not want to spend another week out in wine country if I could help it. Especially with bullets flying.

Once again at the Ryder Estate, I tended to Lila's lunch and medication, and off she went to nap. I decided it was time to take another walk over to the winery and see if anything I'd said to Stephanie had gained traction. She was a difficult one to read, but one never knew, did one?

When I arrived, she was in front of the winery finishing up a conversation with a cute cowboy. His accent was Australian and the dog was a Brittany spaniel. I figured he might be the vineyard manager, and judging by the way their conversation ended, I was right.

The Aussie cowboy and his dog got into a late model pickup and took their leave. Stephanie raised her eyebrows at me. "I came to talk to you some more about your mom," I said. "Have you had any more thoughts about who we might get out here to spend nights at the house with her and run some of her errands?"

Stephanie opened her mouth and closed it. Then she said, "I don't have time to talk about this."

Her obdurate look said more than anything she could have uttered. "Stephanie, this is your mother we're talking about," I said. "I can work with your mom, but it would be better if you and your sisters were involved too, so everyone is comfortable with the arrangements. Maybe the two of us could set up a meeting with Morgan and Regan and your mom, and just figure this thing out. I'm happy to help out, but I do have my own life to get back to".

Stephanie scrunched up her face. I thought she might cry. "No, I won't talk to them," she said. "They want to sell the winery."

"What do you mean? Who wants to sell the winery?"

"Regan. And Morgan. They say they're going to sell the winery when Mom dies."

So that was the problem. At least part of it. "Your mom isn't going to die," I told her. "Her cancer is being successfully treated, and she's a very strong woman. I know your sisters must be concerned, but I think you've misunderstood what they're saying. Meanwhile, your mom needs help now while she's still sick."

Stephanie ran her hand through her greasy hair. "No, I'm right. They say we're going to sell the winery, and I'll just have to find a job somewhere else."

Somebody just shoot me. It just kept getting weirder with this woman. "Okay, I hear you," I said. "But yesterday you told me your mom was going to sell the winery. Your sisters can't sell anything. Even if your mom died, she's not going to let anyone sell the winery out from under you. Your mom owns the winery and she is alive and she needs some help from the family."

"Well, I can't help. I have a winery to run."

I was talking to a door. "Fine, Stephanie," I said. I turned and walked away. "Don't worry about a thing, Stephanie, I'll take care of it," I said to myself as I returned to the house disgruntled.

I looked in on Lila. She was in her usual position, mouth open and sleeping like a babe. I jotted her a quick note and prepared a snack for when she got up, should she awaken before my return. Then I gathered my swimming things, and drove over to the Westerly. Oh, and I made certain the damned door was locked. It was still early in the afternoon, and that pool would feel mighty good on a warm day. I stopped inside to change before hitting the water.

Melody and Angel were chatting in the kitchen, but stopped immediately upon seeing me. "Any more information on last night's bombs bursting in air?" Melody asked.

"It was a single bullet, Melody. But to answer your question, no."

Melody explained the context to Angel, who quickly crossed herself.

"Something goofy is going on in that family, however," I said. I filled them in on the goings-on with Stephanie, and also about how the bullying Regan and Morgan had showed up at the house a couple days previous. "I hate being in the middle of it. It's not good," I concluded.

Melody walked to the refrigerator and brought out a pitcher of iced tea. She poured three glasses full and set them on the table. "I don't like it," she said. "What gives those two the right to go in there and hassle Lila when she's still in such a raw state from James's death? And having to deal with cancer on top of that!"

"And what about their sister, the winemaker?" I said. "If they do sell the place, it's not like she's going to be widely marketable. She's too quirky."

Melody shook her head. "Quirky is a nice way of putting it. And I don't think that woman has had a decent haircut since she graduated high school." Not to mention the manicures, pedicures, and other things Melody would expect of a daughter. Thankfully, she only had boys.

"I don't care about the haircuts," I said. "I've had enough fun out here and I want to go home. Nobody is talking about what's going to happen when I leave. I need someone to step up."

"Maybe she'll be okay," Melody said. "She looked great last night."

"Yes, but she had chemo today. So yesterday is the last best day she'll have for a while, and then she'll do chemo again. I think she still has another six treatments after this one. I can't just leave her by herself if she doesn't have someone to stay there." I turned my attention to Angel. "What do you think, Angel? Do you know anyone who could do what I'm doing for Lila? And maybe more, if she gets sicker?"

Angel sighed and rose from the table. "I may know someone, Senora," she said. "It is terrible about the daughters, yes. And now I go home." I stood up and hugged her. Then she removed her apron, folded it, and carried it into the laundry room off the kitchen. When she emerged with her handbag, she gave us both a nod and left.

"If you don't mind, I'm going to take a swim," I said.

No sooner had the words come out of my mouth, when a black Humvee pulled up at the Carriage House. Uh-oh. My wrestling partners from the vineyard had arrived. "Well, well," said Melody. "This should be interesting."

We stood at the slider and watched as Marv and Pete stepped out of their vehicle and walked to the entrance that led to the apartment above the garage area. They banged on the door, and then entered. We watched, hardly breathing. I felt like a gossipy old lady, but that was just too bad. It wasn't going to stop us from watching. We couldn't ignore something that was part of the unfolding drama of our lives for the past two weeks. We watched for ten minutes. Nothing happened, so we sat down at the round oak table and sipped our tea and waited.

Finally, after what seemed like an age, Marv and Pete, the FBI agents, and Marla all emerged from the door to the Carriage House. We stood up and watched raptly. There was no drama, no Gunfight at the OK Corral. Marv and Pete were handcuffed. The agents wore expressions suggesting dire constipation—probably normal, all things considered. Marla started crying and one of the agents put his arm around her! Jesus! Melody and I looked at each other, and then back at the scene. The two Nevadans were placed in the back of the agents' vehicle. One of the agents pulled the Humvee up next to the Carriage House. And then it was all over.

"Well, well," said Melody again. "I hope they come back and get that damn Humvee. I don't like those things."

I was glad I wouldn't be running into those characters again. I probably wouldn't be so lucky next time. "At least we know where they are now. That's good enough for me," I said.

I spent a blissful hour in the pool, alternately swimming laps and getting out for brief sunbathing breaks. Then, fully refreshed, I drove back to the house to check on Lila. When I arrived, a white Escalade was parked in the drive.

I entered the house to find Regan and Morgan seated at the dining room table with Lila. Regan leaned across the table as if emphasizing a point. Before her on the table were papers and a pen. Lila's face was pale and angry. Morgan fidgeted with a pen. Her face registered alarm when I walked into the room.

Lila looked like she could use an ally, so I decided to make myself at home. "Hi ladies, what brings you out here slumming today?" I said. "I hope I'm not interrupting anything." I walked through the smelly living room and dining room like I owned the place, headed into the kitchen, and poured myself a glass of water, hoping that would give Lila a moment to collect herself.

It did. "Not at all," she called after me. "In fact, I could use your opinion if you have a minute."

I returned to the table and set the glass down. "Sure," I said. "I have all the time in the world. How can I help?" I sat down.

If looks could kill, Regan's glare at me might have done it. Obviously I'd stepped in on something juicy! I looked to Lila for enlightenment. "Regan and Morgan are very anxious for me to put the winery on the market," she said. "So anxious, in fact, that they have come out here with a listing agreement. I wonder if you'd like to weigh in on this."

She hit me broadside. I had no idea what had transpired up until now. "Maybe you could get me up to speed?" I said.

Regan was more than happy to butt in. "Mom, this estate is just too much work for you. We're really worried about you. It would be just so much better for all of us if you'd just let us take care of this. We can find you a beautiful condo in the Pearl. You'll be closer to us."

She laid it on pretty thick. However, I wasn't picking up any worrying about Mom vibes. Rather, my bullshit meter was having a field day. Clearly the girls had an agenda.

Then Morgan piped in. "Yeah, Mom. I'm just so concerned—especially with your health problems. And the winery, too. It's just way too much for you."

Lila took a good look at each of them. "You don't really know what I do around here, or how much," she said. "Neither one of you have come around for nearly five years. And before that you didn't come very often. Since you mentioned the winery, you should be aware that I have very little involvement with that. Stephanie is in charge, and is doing a remarkably good job staying on top of things."

Morgan again. "Yes, but without Daddy, well, you know."

Lila shot her a blazing look. "Know *what*!" It was a challenge, not a question.

"The bi-polar disorder, Mother," said Regan. "She's mentally ill, or have you forgotten?"

"Bi-polar? Since when? You're the one who diagnosed that," said Lila, "As far as I'm concerned, Stephanie is fine. Just because she's not like you doesn't mean she's mentally ill. She loves her job and she's good at it. I know she wouldn't risk losing it. She's as good as anyone out there—and better than most. So I trust her. There isn't an issue."

Well said, Lila.

But Regan wasn't finished. "Don't tell me you haven't noticed that Stephanie has become increasingly withdrawn and erratic."

Lila's face was ashen. I could tell she was enraged, but Regan had managed to hit her worry button. "What are you talking about?"

Regan looked smug. "We've been spending some time with her," she nodded to Morgan. "We've noticed she's really getting weird."

Lila pulled herself together enough to brush them off. "You are talking to the wrong person regarding Stephanie," she said. "Right now, I just want to hear what Emma thinks of your proposal."

All three of them now looked at me.

I assumed an air of nonchalance that I certainly didn't feel. "The general rule for someone in a situation like yours, Lila, is to not make any big decisions for at least a year. You're right at the beginning of the grieving process. On top of that, you need to get your health back on track before you'll really know what's best for you and how you want to live your life now that James is gone."

As much as I disliked what the daughters were pulling, I would have said the exact same thing to anyone else in Lila's position. Grief clouded every decision. It took a year, if not longer, for the grieving person to even know which end was up.

Regan jumped right in. "I think that's very bad advice, Mom." She didn't say why.

Morgan, all pink-cheeked and perspiring, piped in with, "The market is really good right now, Mom. Everything that's been listed out here sells in a heartbeat. There is a lot of money coming into the valley. But, things could change in a year, and we wouldn't get as much."

Lila reacted quickly to the suggestion that her winery was a "we" thing. "Just remember this, young lady. Your father and I started this winery, and we were the owners of this winery until he died. Now *I* own the winery, and I plan to remain its sole owner until my demise. Even without Emma's timely advice, I am not interested in making any changes right now and I'm not going to make any changes in the near future."

She didn't ask them to leave, so I stood. "Would you ladies like to join us for dinner? We probably eat a little early for your tastes, but your mom just had chemo today, and it's important that she stays on her schedule." All bullshit, of course. I knew the invitation would send them out the door, and it did. They scrambled for handbags. Regan stuffed her blasted papers into a briefcase, and they scuttled out of the house like a couple of Dungeness crabs.

I brought Lila a glass of water. She wiped her forehead with a napkin from the table. "Thank God you arrived when you did," she said. "Regan was on the warpath. I think she would have arm-wrestled me into signing that listing agreement. She actually frightened me."

"Did she wake you from your nap?" I asked.

"Yes. She was very abrupt about it. I'm completely distressed."

"So that means she has a key to the house?"

Lila's face changed. She gave me a hard look. "I'm not certain if she has a key, but she very well could."

"Either one or both of your daughters have a key," I said. "I locked up tight when I left the house."

Regan had frightened me too. The woman was possessed. They both were. The question was, what was going on with them? Before we could discuss that, however, Lila surprised me. "I'm going to change my will," she said. "Right here and right now. Tonight. And I want you to witness it."

Probably this would be the time to have some good lawyerly advice. "I think we might want to think about this for a minute," I said. "I think we need to have two witnesses. Let me go check on it."

I hustled down the hall and booted up my laptop. Yes, we needed two witnesses. No, handwritten wills didn't cut it in Oregon. I carried my laptop back to the dining room and set it on the table.

"Here's the deal," I said. "We need to get someone else over here to co-witness whatever changes you're making. And, it needs to be a printed document. I think I can get Melody to come over this evening. But first you have to eat something."

I opened Word and placed the computer in front of Lila. "Here. I'll fix dinner and you compose until it's time to eat. Then, I assume I can go over to the winery and make copies?"

"No need to do that," Lila said. "We have a home office downstairs." She positioned her hands over the keyboard. I brought out a cranberry juice cocktail and some cheese and crackers to give her strength. I called Melody to invite her over for dinner and a witnessing. Then I got to work on a simple pasta dish and a salad.

By the time Melody pulled into the driveway, Lila had just finished drafting the codicil to her will. I took the laptop to the basement office, where I plugged it in to the Ryder printer and printed it out. While it was printing, I read the thing. No reason not to that I could see. I mean, as long as we were going to witness its signing in a few minutes. Basically, Lila removed Regan as executor and named me in her place. She hadn't even asked me yet, but what the hell. It would work during this time of emergency. Instead of going straight to the daughters, all the estate's assets were to be managed by Dan Wyatt, financial guru and Melody's beloved husband, at the executor's discretion.

I said a silent prayer that unknown someones would not start firing bullets at my house if the contents of the amended will became known. And then it struck me. *The daughters.* Why hadn't one of us thought seriously of them before now? They were badly behaved, greedy, and rude. Not that it made them murderers, per se. But they might have tried to scare their mom. If they were desperate enough—and I was certain that financial desperation fit into their winery-selling plans somewhere. Otherwise, why butt in? And who, besides the Ryder daughters, would have an overwhelming need to get rid of Max Weatherman, whose finaglings stood to devalue the Ryder Estate property by putting its water supply in jeopardy?

Goodness me! When looking for motive, one always must ask the question, who stands to gain from getting so-and-so out of the way. Max clearly was a pain in the old wazoo for all the Ryders. But since two of the three sisters were scheming to sell the property, why not pop him off? It would save them having to hassle with him later on down the road.

But if so, how? And again, where was he?

Settle down, I told myself. Murder is an extreme way of dealing with a problem. Still, we all know people have killed for less than their share of a multi-million-dollar property. And why not take a potshot at the house while they were at it? Shake Mom up enough and she'll be racing to get out of there. It was something to ponder. Something to look into, and maybe even run past Florian Craig. He seemed to know his way around the scene.

I carried the papers back upstairs. Melody let us know, the moment I emerged from the basement, that business would have to wait. "We can deal with that stuff later, honey," she said. "I'm ready to eat the ass off an alligator!"

I threw some pasta into a pot of simmering water and tossed the salad. Melody opened herself a bottle of wine and Lila grated the Parmesan. Within minutes, our feast was on the table.

Lila was very specific in her verbal instructions to us. Whatever happened with her, she had effectively disarmed her two older daughters from any direct access to the Ryder assets. Stephanie still had control of making certain the winery was run properly, but Lila's income and the money that came into the family coffers on a quarterly basis could not be accessed by any of the daughters. If Stephanie were to become unable to run the winery, then control would revert to Lila if she was still alive, or the executor, who would then find suitable replacements for winemaker and general manager. It seemed to cover the bases.

"I'd give money to see their faces when those two realize what Lila has done," I told Melody as I walked her to out to her car two hours later. Lila already had said goodnight and retired to her room.

We said our goodbyes under a lovely crescent moon. I then locked everything, checked on Lila, and padded down the hall to my own bedroom, where I took up notebook and pen and began writing my thoughts about Regan and Morgan, and Lila's changes.

CHAPTER 17

The next morning my coffee making duties were interrupted by the sounds of puking. I hurried into Lila's bedroom to see if she needed anything. "This chemo's kicking my butt," she said.

"Anything I can do?" I asked.

"Not really. Just leave me alone for a while." I went back into the kitchen. Lila spent the morning in bed while I tried to figure out something that would calm things down. Good old black tea with lemon seemed to work the best.

"These cocktails have made me sick before," said Lila when I checked on her mid-morning. "But I think the aggravation of my daughters is what makes me the sickest. I don't think I was a bad mother. But look at the way they turned out. James has been dead a mere two weeks, and already they are figuring out some way to get their paws on our property."

"Something must be going on," I said.

Lila scrunched up her mouth, then said, "I don't know what it could be. They both have great jobs. Morgan is short of money, and always has been, but that's the way she lives. Regan is just the opposite, and she makes a lot of it. Of course, they started pressuring us five years ago. That's part of the reason we're having these problems now. But I don't understand it. What makes them think they have the right?"

I shrugged. Nothing more to say about that situation. It had nothing to do with me. Who could imagine I'd be walking into a hornet's nest when I agreed to help Lila? The very last thing in the world I wanted to do was to stir up the shit with those sisters.

An hour later, Lila began moving about. "I think I can get up now," she said. "I'm feeling a bit better." It was just past noon. I helped her into the shower and assumed my position outside the door. Ten minutes later I left her to get dressed while I made something for her lunch. It was starting out to be a very long day. However, half an egg salad sandwich later, Lila decided to head back to bed. "Go for your swim," she told me. "You've earned it. I just need to take it easy, but I'll be fine."

I was only too glad to oblige. I watched her take her slew of medications, tucked her in, and grabbed my swimsuit. I needed a couple hours to just veg and think about things. The main topic for today was to find a caregiver type who could do what I'd been doing all week and then some. The goal was to bring my brief nursing career to an abrupt but peaceful end. I wanted to be able to feel good about leaving, but leaving was the goal. And leaving soon. I didn't enjoy the family fuss. Even less, the gunshot the previous night. Just get me out of here was my theme song.

The other item on my thinking agenda had to do with the two wicked sisters. I was pretty sure Melody would have opinions to share on that one.

On the way out the door, I once again noted the smell in the front rooms of the house. It was worse. I'd talked to Lucila. I planned to smudge the blasted place, but other than that I was out of ideas. For all I knew, a rat had burrowed into the walls of the house, died, and finally had ripened to near perfection. Once again, not my circus, not my monkey. Leaving would give me respite from the stink. Somebody else could worry about a rat or colony of rats between the walls.

I threw my swimming gear into the car, started off, and bounced through the Dundee Hills toward the Westerly. It was such a gift to have that haven to go to. My discomfort with the drama in Lila's life was increasing faster than my spirit of acceptance could keep up with it. The pool would improve my attitude. Something about the water, being outdoors in it, freed me and restored my soul.

As I pulled into my usual parking spot, Melody emerged from the garden with a basket of ripe tomatoes, Winston by her side. "Well, hello there, you old sage hen," she said. "What brings you out today?" Winston ran to greet me and I patted him on the head.

I removed my gear from the car and straightened up, running a hand through my hair. "Same old," I said. "Lila's having a difficult day, but she perked up a little and finally ate something. Now she's napping and I need a break."

"Well, come on in and change, make yourself at home," Melody said.

"I don't know what I'd do if I had to stay there all day," I said. "After those nasty girls came by yesterday, I've just had it. I realize that awful things happen, but I don't need to be in the middle of them. It's so hard to watch that stuff go down. I was happy to sign Lila's codicil, but I want no more to do with their family drama."

And then, as if out of the blue, Melody said, "What if it helped you solve the crime?"

I stopped in my tracks. "What do you mean?"

Melody shrugged. "Just that. You're sitting on a time bomb with that family. What's the story behind the story?"

She sounded like me. In fact, I had wondered that myself. "Do you think…?" The sentence hung there. Once again I thought, the girls. What about those *girls*?

Melody started up the steps to the deck and kitchen. I just stood there shocked at the possibility. "I don't know what to think, honey" she said over her shoulder. "But something weird's going on up there."

I trotted up the stairs behind her.

"You get yourself out by the pool and relax a while," Melody said. "I'll bring out some sweet tea and join you in a bit."

I changed into my swimsuit and walked out to the pool. I spread my towel on one of the chaise lounges, situated myself, and opened my book. But I couldn't concentrate. My mind was spinning like a roulette wheel. I set aside the book and slipped into the pool. The water was tepid and silky on my skin. I rolled over and floated on my back, but I soon tired of it. Agitated, I swam up and down the pool—breast-stroke, side-stroke, breast-stroke, back-stroke—until I had worked out the stress. Then I climbed out of the pool and toweled off.

I was applying sunscreen when Melody sashayed across the broad lawn as only Melody can do. She bore a tray with glasses of iced tea and what looked like a plate of yummy cookies. Immediately I was all attention.

She set the refreshments on an umbrella table and plopped herself in a chair in the shade of the umbrella. "Snacks are served," she said. I was right there and into the cookies before she had the words out of her mouth. She grabbed a one and bit off half of it. "If we didn't have such good metabolism, we'd each weigh three hundred pounds," she observed.

I helped myself to a glass of the tea and sat down next to her. "I feel better," I said.

Melody munched another cookie and took a swig of tea. "I'm glad. If last evening was any indication, things are pretty tense up there."

"Those daughters are just insufferable," I said. "At least the older two. Stephanie is a loose cannon in her own right, but at least she's not trying to destroy the very thing her parents spent forty years building."

"I know you've had your mind on other things," said Melody. "But while you were swimming I went on line to see what I could see. And guess what?" She paused for effect.

After a few seconds, I shot her a look. "Well? Are you really going to make me guess?"

Melody sipped her tea. "Guess who was disbarred two months ago and no longer is able to practice law in Oregon?"

I slammed my glass down on the table. Tea flew out onto it. "Nooo! Really?"

"Oh, yes," said Melody. "Messing around with clients' funds. Comingling them, or whatever. Basically, she had her hand in the cookie jar, and the Oregon Bar Association just hates it when that happens. We're out here in the sticks, so we didn't hear about it. But it did make *The Oregonian*—just probably not the edition we get in Yamhill County. Regan is jobless in Portland."

"With a very big lifestyle to support," I said.

"And that membership at the MAC," said Melody.

"Tsk, tsk. Well, at least now we know why she's so eager to unload a winery that isn't hers to sell."

We momentarily forgot about the cookies.

Then I thought of something else. "She's married, isn't she?" I asked.

Melody pondered the question. "Last I knew," she said. "But these things have a way of changing quickly when things are headed south."

"Well, what does he do? She wouldn't have married someone she considered beneath her."

"I think he's a professor at Portland State," said Melody. "He's got a good job, but not nearly lucrative enough to get them into the MAC."

"But it's not like they're going to starve," I said.

"Depending on their lifestyle, and their debts, it could get pretty rough," Melody said. "She pulled in a lot of money. It's not like she can go out and get another job as a top flight trial lawyer. Her career is over."

"When did it happen?"

"Back in June sometime. I'm surprised that word didn't get around out here."

I snorted and smeared on some more sunscreen. "Few out here would notice," I said. "She hasn't been a part of the community for at least fifteen years, she probably uses her married name, and everybody's thinking of other things. Lila doesn't even know. Or if she does, she's given no indication." Indeed, she'd seemed bewildered by her daughters' avarice and rudeness.

And then I told Melody about the murder weapon. Maybe I shouldn't have, but it was weighing on me and I had to tell someone. "Oh my God," she said, hand on her heart. "Do you feel safe up there?"

"Well, it's not like Lila's a murderer," I said. "Anyone could have gone in there and taken that knife." My mind was going crazy with the possibility that Regan may have murdered her father. Or put one of her sisters up to it. That would be more her style. Yes, it was a little far-fetched, but then most murders are.

"Humph," said Melody. She took another sip of tea and set the glass down. "You don't really *know* that Lila's not a murderer.

I grabbed another cookie. "Well, no. But I'm betting against it."

"All I'm saying is that you need to keep all the possibilities on the table."

We hung out by the pool for another fifteen minutes. When I'd had enough, I grabbed my towel and sunscreen and we and headed back to the house. I changed my clothes, still ruminating on Regan and her recent disgrace.

When I returned to the kitchen to say goodbye, I noticed Melody had poured herself a stiff one. "It's five o'clock somewhere," she said when she noticed my stare. She took a sip of something that looked like Scotch.

"Knock yourself out," I said. "Just so long as you don't end up like me."

"To be honest, this business with the knife has me worried for your safety," she said. "Would it help if I came up and spent the night?"

I laughed. It was a bit hollow, but a laugh nonetheless. "Don't worry, Melody. I think I'll be fine. You know, Lila is the last person on earth who would kill anyone," I said. "I think she's got a real concern about those two older daughters, though. You should have seen the way they behaved."

Melody shook her head. "As I said earlier, some weird shit is going on up there, honey. You got beat up. And there was the gunshot. And now you tell me about the knife and you're not concerned? I don't like it one bit."

I gave her a quick hug. "I'm leaving now, but I'll be back," I said. "And I've made up my mind. I'm going to go home by the middle of next week. I've had enough. I'll do what I can to help find a replacement, but that is not my responsibility. I've had enough of this entire business, trust me."

I was sick of cooking, so I did what I'd promised to do several nights ago. I stopped by my favorite hamburger joint, purchased two cheeseburgers, a large order of fries, and a large strawberry milk shake. While I waited for my order, I dug out the card of Sheriff Deputy Doug Haymore and dialed his direct line. He answered on the first ring.

I identified myself and cut to the chase. "I've got some information which hopefully will be of interest," I said. I outlined the visits from Regan and Morgan, and their forceful attempts to talk Lila into selling the Ryder property. Just in case Regan hadn't told him, I also mentioned her recent disgrace. I mean why not? It had been in *The Oregonian* so it wasn't a secret.

When I'd finished, he said, "Duly noted, Ms. Golden. Thank you for your information." And that was it. He gave no indication whether the news I gave him was new, or if he already was on top of it. And such are the rewards of doing one's civic duty. I returned to Lila's house with a clear conscience and a bag full of burgers and fries.

Lila put away most of the milkshake and nibbled at the burger and fries. I managed to devour my cheeseburger and cleaned up the fries. The smell in the living room had gotten worse, to the point that I could no longer keep quiet about it. "I think you may have a dead rat or rats in one of your walls," I told Lila. "Surely you've noticed that awful smell."

She looked at me without concern. "Oh, really?" she said. "Oh dear. Well, the chemo does affect my sense of smell. But I certainly can get someone out to look at it in the next day or two. I don't need any dead rats in the house."

We were at a bit of a loss after dinner. I made tea for Lila and a cup of coffee for myself, but we avoided the deck. It remained to be seen if someone actually was shooting at us the previous night or if it was all a big mistake. I was not interested in testing our luck.

While we sat in the living room, I told her of my plans. "I've been happy to help you this past week," I said, "but the time has come for me to return to Portland. I'm planning to leave by Tuesday or Wednesday, so it would be a good thing for us to find someone in the next day or two who can step in where I left off."

Lila's face registered regret. "Oh, I wish you could stay longer," she said. "This has gone so well for me. I feel so safe." Despite an attack on my person not fifty yards from her house, and a bullet in her ceiling.

"I love it out here, believe me, and I've been happy to pitch in," I lied, but it was only a partial lie. I felt good about how much I'd been able to help Lila, and it was a lovely place to stay, but at this point all I wanted was a speedy exit. "However, I do have a life in Portland that needs my attention. Angel, over at the Westerly, knows someone whose daughter is studying at Linfield to be a nurse. Maybe we should check to see if she'd be available for overnights. I imagine a student would be really happy to have a room like the one I'm staying in plus a little cash." There. I'd laid the groundwork. I could even make the telephone call if that was required. I'd basically do whatever it took to facilitate my departure.

Lila nodded and mulled it over. "If you have the number, I'll call her in the morning," she said. "Now, I'm going to the bedroom to watch a little television and make it an early night."

Her nights were always early. While she was doing her evening rituals, I prepared the medications and a little snack for the bedside table. After she took her pills, I said goodnight and retreated through the stinky living room to my own lair. I had work to do.

First I called Rob Grimes at his home. "Have you heard anything more about the Weatherman BMW?" I asked, after we dispensed with pleasantries. "It's been on my mind for some reason."

Rob, as always, was forthcoming. "The car was squeaky clean," he said. "From the look of things, it was running and in gear.

It just went over the side of the road in first gear with the motor on, and the motor continued to run until it ran out of gas. No footprints, no nothing. It was wiped clean as a whistle, but there was no evidence of blood or anything else that had been cleaned up."

"Interesting. Any idea how long it had been there?"

"From the look of the underbrush, it had been there a few days before someone spotted it. It would probably still be there if some bicyclist hadn't stopped at the very place it went over to fix a flat."

I thanked Rob, then told him about my little rumble in the vineyard, the gunshot, and the Ryder daughters' eagerness to get their hands on Lila's property. "Thanks for the information," he said. "I hadn't heard any of that stuff."

"Well, at least the creeps from Las Vegas presumably are now in jail," I said. "Somebody from forensics came up while I was out yesterday and dug the bullet out of the ceiling. And there is a smell in the house that won't go away. It's so weird up here that I just want to go home."

"As far I know, your Henderson friends are still in custody. But who knows for how long," Rob said.

"Let's hope they stay there for a while," I said. "I didn't want to tell the detectives about being beat up by them, but I'm glad I did. I also told them about the daughters. You already know they came up here the night the shot was fired at the house."

"What did they say after your information dump?"

"Thank you," I said. "What else could they say?"

"Not much," Rob agreed. And with that we hung up.

It was still early. I was tempted to go out and wander in the vineyard—it was such a lovely evening—but if something was going on out there, it would be better if I wasn't a part of it. I left my room long enough to brew a cup of herbal tea to sip on while I wrote. I also made certain everything was locked up tight, Then I returned to my room to settle in with the notebook.

I thought, and wrote, about Regan and Morgan. What awful people. And yet I was only about halfway there on thinking of them as murder suspects. What wrongs had their father ever done to them, real or imagined, to deserve the kind of revenge, the act of pure hatred that had been dealt him in that outhouse? He had his flaws, certainly, but I very much doubted that he'd ever done anything to them to cause their anger or disappointment, short of perhaps missing some of their soccer games.

But there was that rift. Five years is a long time to stay angry, a long time to avoid seeing one's parents. Family quarrels could be nasty, but often the things family members stayed angriest about with each other were the types of things that outsiders found trivial or amusing. Knowing James as I did, I was certain there had been no type of meanness or unfairness toward any of the three daughters.

One of them was running the winery. As Lila had said to them earlier, the parents had given each of them everything they needed to assure the best futures possible, including financing advanced degrees in teaching, law, and enology and viticulture.

It only made sense that James blew up with they made the preposterous suggestion that he and Lila turn the financial management of the winery over to them. James was not a man who would ever retire. He loved what he did. Anyone of average perception soon would have realized the error of their ways, but not those two. From what I'd seen, it appeared their resentments had festered and grown. Since his death, that seems to have made them feel even more entitled.

Max Weatherman was still missing in action, but as Florian had pointed out, he was probably dead. I wouldn't believe it, however, until there was a body. He could be lurking in places such as the Ryder vineyard, making mischief such as shooting at us on a warm summer eve. Or he even, I suppose, could have fed a Cayman Islands bank account for the past several years and decided it was time to run off with some sweet young thing, leave Marla hanging out to dry, while he retired in anonymity. Why not?

What about other suspects? If there were some, nobody had told me about them, nor were they likely to do so. The thugs still loomed as a big question mark. If they hadn't still been looking for

Max Weatherman, my money would be on them killing him. But they seemed as baffled as anyone else that he could not be found. Other than that, there was not a single other person who came to mind as a likely candidate.

And then a new and horrifying thought struck me. It was back to Lila. What if she had killed James? The authorities had taken her passport. The murder weapon came from the knife drawer in her very own kitchen. She had been alone on the night of the murder, presumably because she wasn't feeling well enough to attend the Salmon Bake. That wasn't much of an alibi.

I mulled it over. Could she have summoned the strength to hang out, perhaps for hours, watching, while she waited for James to make a trip to the latrine? Probably not. Did she have the physical strength to stab him, and then get clean away without drawing attention before I—or someone else—inadvertently showed up at the murder scene? Good question.

Lila was not a healthy woman. To pull this off, for starters, she would have had to be nurturing an epic resentment. It happened with married couples, as I myself can attest, it rarely ended with murder. She'd also need to feel a whole lot better than she did at any time since I'd been staying with her. She couldn't walk very far or be on her feet for more than just a few minutes. She just plain didn't have the juice. She would have needed an accomplice. And even if she had, what on earth could be the motive?

I put my pen down and closed the notebook. Then I just sat there in bed for a few minutes, sipping my now cold tea and thinking. I'd felt a twinge of discomfort around Lila during the past twenty-four hours. My feeling had nothing to do with anything that had happened or been said. It was just there, my intuition like a determined dog gnawing on a bone in my subconscious. The feeling was at odds with my conscious mind, and yet it remained lodged there and it wouldn't go away. Could it possibly be Lila, or was it someone else?

And back to those two from Las Vegas? The FBI agents had hauled them off for some reason. Had they perhaps been responsible for the suspicious death in Henderson? Had they come up here to continue with their murdering ways, or were they really just looking for Weatherman in order to nudge him back to Nevada? I'd had direct experience with them. It had been rough, scary, and altogether unpleasant. Yes, I actually could see them killing someone.

I jumped out of bed and paced around the room. I thought of calling Melody, but it was too late. And where was Florian Craig when a girl needed him? In Portland, no doubt, having sex with my good friend. Whatever was bothering me would have to wait until tomorrow. Irritated, I returned to bed and turned out the light.

CHAPTER 18

The next morning dawned normally. I was awake by six, topping off an early week. I wrapped myself in my bathrobe and trundled down the hall to make the coffee. The normalcy of the day ended as I neared the living room.

The smell hit me like a wall. Something was dead in this very house, and it was a lot bigger than a rat!

I walked into the living room, threw open the doors and window, turned on all the lights, and began looking around. I looked behind and under furniture. I poked around every little nook and cranny, wondering if some raccoon or other sick animal had somehow made its way into the house when a door was left ajar and then perished behind an *objet d'art* or a chair. My mind went wild. What was I even looking for?

I stared at the walls, as if hoping they would provide me a clue. I ran my hands down the walls. I even smelled them. And then I looked over at the settee. Big. Outrageously beautiful. *Storage area under the seat.*

I took a couple tentative steps toward it. The smell, if anything, worsened. Suddenly I knew that it was too early in the morning for what I was going to find in there. I also knew I had to man up and get it over with. I reached down and grabbed the protruding cloth tab. I lifted the seat.

Inside the settee was a chamber straight out of hell. Before me lay a rotted corpse that had been covered with lime, probably when it had been stowed in the settee. As far as odor control was concerned, the lime had had its day. It consisted of a thick, ashen layer that covered the body and face and had settled over its time in the settee to roughly outline the body. The corpse, that of a medium-height male—let's just call him Max Weatherman, because the sleeve of a Tommy Bahama Hawaiian shirt stuck out on one side of the mess along with a tasseled loafer at the far end—had turned to mush.

I stifled a scream. Sickened, I dropped the seat and ran down the hall to the nearest bathroom, where I proceeded to puke my guts out. I finished my retching, grabbed the air freshener, and headed back to the living room. I sprayed it everywhere, then ran out onto the deck to get away from the smell. Then, still shaking, I grabbed my phone and dialed Detective Haymore's cell phone number.

It rang three or four times before he answered. I could tell I'd woken him from a sound slumber. I quickly identified myself and said, "You've got to get up here. I've found Max Weatherman."

Suddenly he sounded wide awake. "Where are you?"

"Lila Ryder's house." I hung up.

What to do next. I went back inside and was looking around somewhat wildly when Lila emerged from the bedroom. "What on earth is going on out here?" she said. "Why are all the lights on and what is that awful smell?"

At least her olfactories were finally working. "There's a dead person in your settee," I said.

Her hand went straight to her heart. She stared at me as if I'd just stepped off a UFO. "A *what*? How is that even possible?" Her hand dropped to her side. Still staring at me she said, "Oh, I get it. You're joking. Ha ha."

I walked a few steps closer to her. She looked as if she might back away. "Seriously, Lila. Max Weatherman is in your settee. He's very dead, and from the looks of him, he's been there for quite a while."

Lila looked at the settee as if it might attack her. "Oh dear God!" she cried. "How on earth did he get there?"

I watched her for signs of prevarication. As far as I could tell, there were none. "I'd be willing to bet he was killed right here in your living room," I said. "Somebody covered him in a lot of lime, so we didn't start smelling him until he got really ripe." I had no idea how long that could be, but since I'd been smelling him for several days, probably about as long as he had been missing.

Lila looked at me and then back at the settee. She looked as if she might throw up, even though she hadn't actually looked at the body. "Are you sure it's him?"

"Reasonably," I said. "I can't see his face, but he's wearing a Tommy Bahama Hawaiian shirt and tassel loafers."

Lila shuddered. "I absolutely don't believe this," she said.

"I called our favorite detectives," I said. "They'll be here momentarily."

She groped for a chair. "I need to sit down. How long have you known about this situation?"

"Approximately fifteen minutes."

Lila dropped into her favorite chair and covered her face with her hands. "What have I done to deserve this life?" she moaned. I think the body in her favorite piece of furniture was the proverbial straw. She started crying like her heart would break.

I hated to interrupt what seemed to be a perfectly justifiable meltdown, but John Law was on his way. "Lila, we're going to have company any minute. Do you want your wig?"

She groped at her head, then rose from the chair and scurried into the bedroom. Lila didn't like to be seen without her hair. In fact, this was one of the very few times I'd seen her wigless. I went into the kitchen and started making a pot of coffee. I, at least, needed something to give me strength.

No sooner had the coffee started brewing than the doorbell rang and in walked Jeffers and Haymore, both in their suits and looking freshly scrubbed. They looked tired and grumpy as well, but at least they didn't have a rotting corpse destroying their finest furniture. "Come in, detectives," I said. "Let me ruin your day."

They walked in, noses twitching. The place absolutely reeked, despite all the open doors and windows. Lila emerged from her bedroom dressed and bewigged. Except for the expression on her face, she looked sensational.

"Where is he?" Jeffers demanded.

I walked to the settee and opened the seat to reveal our late friend Weatherman. "Right here, gentlemen. I'm no expert, but I'm guessing he's been here ever since the night he didn't return to the Westerly."

The men covered their noses and mouths with handkerchiefs and advanced toward the settee. They leaned over and looked in. Haymore squatted down for a closer look. "Call forensics," he muttered over his shoulder. Jeffers pulled out his phone and began punching numbers.

Haymore stood, closed the settee, and backed away. "When did you find him?" he asked me.

"A few minutes ago, just before I called you," I said.

Then he turned to Lila. "What do you know about this, ma'am?"

Lila, if possible, looked whiter than her normal pallor. "Why, nothing," she said. "I was in bed. I heard noise out here and came out to see what it was. Emma told me there was a body in my settee."

"You didn't notice the smell earlier?"

"No. Emma asked me about a bad odor last night, but I think the chemotherapy has affected my sense of smell. Until this morning, I didn't notice anything."

"Humph," said Haymore.

Pocketing his phone, Jeffers moved in next to Haymore. "Who has access to your home besides yourself, ma'am?"

A panicky look came over Lila as she began to see where the questioning could lead. She looked around until she found me and her eyes locked with mine. "Why, lots of people. I believe my daughters each have a key to the house. My housekeeper. Emma, while she's here. But I usually don't lock the door," she said. "It's always been so safe out here."

Haymore shook his head. "I want you to start locking your doors, ma'am," he said. "If you go down the hall to the bathroom, lock your doors. It is not necessarily safe out here. Do you understand me?"

Lila nodded. Her eyes brimmed with tears.

"Our forensic team will be here in approximately thirty minutes," said Jeffers. "We are going to need full access to the house. They will remove your furniture item here with the body in it. I doubt you're going to want it back. We will be conducting some tests, and also going through the rest of the house. It will be much better for everyone if you are somewhere else. Do you have some place you can go for a few hours?"

I took Lila by the arm and gently escorted her back to her chair, where she landed with a sigh. Then I marched into the kitchen and began some serious bustling. I filled the water pot and turned it on for tea. Then I poured three cups of coffee and carried two of them to Haymore and Jeffers, who were standing on the far side of the living room near the slider and fresh air, conversing in hushed tones.

Back in the kitchen I scrambled an egg and toasted a piece of bread for Lila's breakfast. I poured juice, and counted out her pills. I brewed a strong cup of tea, placed everything on a tray, and carried it to her where she sat. I sat next to her for a couple minutes, watching her poke at her food. After she'd managed a few bites, she took her medications. I left her to regroup with her tea while I returned to the kitchen.

What was next? I wondered as I tidied the work area and put away the breakfast things. How were we, or more probably they, going to get to the bottom of this awful mess? Would that ghastly smell go away once the settee was removed, or had it soaked through, and into the floor boards, to linger as a horrific reminder of a murder most likely committed on the premises? The horror.

The detectives sipped their coffee and continued with their conversation. I grabbed my coffee mug and repaired to my bedroom, where I placed a call to Melody at the Westerly. "Houston, we've got a great big problem," I said when she picked up the phone.

CHAPTER 19

Lila managed to shower before the forensics people arrived. Once she was out of the shower and getting herself ready for the day, I went out into the living room to talk to the detectives.

"What, if anything, should we do next?" I asked them.

"Nothing for the moment," Haymore said. "I want you both to do what you normally do around here when you return home later today. Do not tell anyone about finding the body. Keep all the windows and doors shut and locked. But, other than that, just follow your normal routine."

Jeffers entered the conversation. "Keep your phone with you at all times," he said. "Don't be waiting for answers right away. We have no way of knowing how long it will be before we have any results from forensics. Some things we may know by tonight, but others will take more time."

"Basically, we need more information before we can move forward," said Haymore. "Of course you want answers right now, but it will take a while. We'll be in touch when there is news we are able to pass on to you."

I felt myself going short of breath. I held up my hands in front of me. Like, stop already. "I need to get out of here," I said. My brain felt foggy. I was trying to breathe. "That's the bottom line. When can I leave? I've had enough." Did I say it or think it? My knees buckled.

The next thing I knew, I was on my back with two men on their knees beside me. They were blurry. "Wake up, Ms. Golden. Wake up!" one of them said. He was slapping my hand.

"Oh, good Lord, is she all right?" It was a woman's voice, cracked with concern.

"She's fine. She just fainted." It was Jeffers.

Suddenly I remembered where I was. I tried to push myself up, but a large hand pushed me back down. "Lie still and just breathe normally for a minute," said Haymore.

I'd had a little bout of the vapors, as my granny used to call it. I didn't want to move. I closed my eyes and breathed deeply, slowly. Someone placed a blanket over me and a pillow under my head. At least I hadn't hit my head. I felt okay, just tired and mushy. It had been the stress, I told myself as I lay there for a few minutes, relaxing, waiting. I could hear people talking, but it was all just distant, jumbled words.

Then the activity level quickened. Something more was happening. More noise, more people. I opened my eyes and pushed myself to a sitting position. People entered the house dressed in white haz-mat suits and disposable booties. They carried cameras and other equipment. The forensics team had arrived.

Unsteadily I made it to my feet and grabbed the arm of Lila's chair. Where was Lila? Haymore and Jeffers gave directions to the new arrivals. They clustered near the settee. A wave of nausea rolled through me as I remembered.

And then I remembered it was time to go. Melody was expecting us at the Westerly. I packed up Lila's pills and my swimsuit. Lila emerged from the bedroom with her book. The detectives were too caught up in their work to tell me I was unfit to drive. A few minutes later we were being greeted by Melody and escorted into the Westerly's large, homey kitchen.

Winston barked and Melody clucked around us as we entered the kitchen. "I'm so glad you're here," she said. "Make yourselves at home. Angel has a treat for us. We can make a day of it."

Forget that, I thought. I just wanted a nap. Lila collapsed in a chair at the round oak table. Angel came over and hugged me. "I am so sorry, Senora," she told me.

I hugged her back. Yes, I was sorry too. Finding another body like that had created a PTSD moment. I really didn't want to go back to that house at all. But here we were, Saturday morning, all together, and I was wondering what to do with Lila. Instead of whining about my traumas, I tried to put myself in her place. It was her house. She couldn't just walk away from it. She was sick. It was a complete nightmare.

This morning Melody was perfect pitch. "Lila, honey, let me make you a nice cup of tea," she said. "Then, if you want, you can just go up to Emma's suite. I designed it for special folks. I never rent it out. You must be just beat from all the stress."

Lila's face brightened. "Why Melody, that would be perfect. I really do need to lie down for a while."

Within a few minutes, tea and coffee were served. Angel offered us blueberry muffins, and a good time was had by all. We even enjoyed a few laughs around the table before Melody showed Lila up to my room.

Then, as I was pouring myself a second cup of coffee and even thinking about eating another muffin, Melody was back at the table with fire in her eye. "Now just what in the Sam Hell is going on up there at Lila's place?" she said. "I want to hear everything."

I told her in detail about the sickening mess in the settee, my little fainting fit, and the forensics people arriving with all their gear. "I think Lila can abandon hope of ever seeing that settee again," I said. For some reason, the piece of furniture was important to me—perhaps as a symbol of a genteel life that had been turned on its ear.

"The detectives think Weatherman was murdered at the house. So I guess my next question is, by whom?"

"Well, it couldn't have been Lila," Melody said with conviction.

That had been my first thought too. "The thing is, in her condition she was the one at the house almost all the time," I said. "It's not like she was out shopping or lunching with friends. If he was killed in her house, there's a high probability that she was there."

Melody looked shocked. "Well, I just don't think she could do it," she said.

"Mentally or physically?" I asked.

Melody thought for a minute. "Either one. She's never shown any signs of aggression. James practically used her as a door mat most of the time. And she's not physically strong enough."

"If Max Weatherman was up there and getting in her face, I think she probably could have shot him," I said. "Physically, I mean. If she had the opportunity to surprise him, she even could have stabbed him. She's a tough cookie in her own way. But you're right. She's very compromised physically because of her illness. And there's no way she could have gotten him into that settee and cleaned up what must have been a horrific mess on top of it. It would have wiped her out for days."

"Of course we don't yet know how he died."

"That's true," I said. "I cannot picture Lila with a gun."

"Not very lady-like," Melody agreed. "So that leaves the rest of them."

I started counting. One and two were the weasel and his sidekick. "The FBI has our friends from New Jersey in custody," I said. "So there go two suspects who were up to no good and were looking for him." Third finger. "There's Lila, but not without an accomplice and a lot more fire in her gut than I've seen to date." Which led me to the fourth and fifth fingers. "It could have been Regan, or Morgan, or both of them together."

"Or," said Melody, "Regan and Morgan without her. Maybe one of them took her on an errand."

"They live in Portland and Beaverton," I said. "How would they know he was going to be there?"

Melody tapped her fingers on the table. "They set up a meeting," she said. "Then one of them took Lila somewhere for a while."

Suddenly I had a thought. "Where does Stephanie fit into all this?" I wondered.

Melody shook her head. "Well, I don't think she's a greedy bitch like those other two, but she's definitely a wild card," she said.

I took a sip of my now tepid coffee. "I don't know anything about Stephanie," I said. "Does anyone? Do *you*?"

"The one thing I know about Stephanie," said Melody, "is that she's always *there.*

Which told me almost everything about her that I needed to know.

CHAPTER 20

With little to do but kill time until the forensics team was finished scouring Lila's house, I made a lazy day of it. I helped Melody clean up the kitchen from the guests' breakfast while Angel dug in on her cooking and baking activities. We all chatted amiably. I tiptoed upstairs a couple of times to check on Lila. My room obviously agreed with her. She was conked out and even snoring on my second visit.

I thanked Melody profusely for letting us come over and intrude upon her day.

She brushed me off with, "What else were you going to do, honey? Sit by the side of the road?"

I offered to help her with other chores, but again she brushed me off. "Haven't you had about enough trouble for one day?" she said. "Go outside and pick me some tomatoes. It will help you relax. And take this stinkin' dog with you. That will be all I ask for the rest of the day. You're free to play in the pool. I can keep an eye on Lila."

I whistled for Winston, who appeared from under the table ready to go. Melody gave me a basket and her big floppy hat. I walked across a broad lawn with Winston trotting beside me, to

Dan's spectacular vegetable garden. There I aimlessly picked tomatoes until the basket was heavy with the ripe, aromatic fruit. Then we returned to the kitchen—Winston to take up his position under the table, and I to change into my swimsuit.

Out in the pool I snagged a bright orange foam noodle and floated comfortably for an indeterminate amount of time. Once again, I had the place to myself. It was cool, quiet, and relaxing. Somewhere on the far side of the Westerly a lawnmower hummed. The sun warmed my back and shoulders, and I was able, in a very short time, to put the morning behind me, to just drift with my thoughts and no interruptions. I thought about silly things from my childhood. I thought of my garden. I thought of Cat and Florian. After a time, I realized that I needed to touch base with Florian. It had been a couple days. I hadn't heard from Cat either—no surprise, as she had both a job and a new boyfriend to occupy her time.

And then I thought about the morning. I reviewed it again and again. It had been horrible, especially for Lila. But I was the one who fainted. I still felt a bit shaky from that, but having the opportunity to just paddle in the pool seemed to help. I'd be myself again in no time.

After a while, I emerged from the water and sprawled facedown on a chaise lounge, but I couldn't relax. My head continued to spin with the morning's events, not to mention those of the past few days. So many balls to juggle up there between my ears. Who knew where they'd all land? One thing for certain, though—a pattern to the events, some seemingly unrelated, was beginning to appear. I was sure there would be an answer soon.

Back in the kitchen, I noticed it was after one o'clock. I had made good my time in the pool. Melody bustled about the kitchen while Angel plied Lila with Mexican comfort food. Lila, smiling, looked like a different person than the one in her living room earlier that morning. I changed into my clothes and returned to the kitchen to find out what everyone was eating. The darkness and horror of the morning managed to dissipate in this homey kitchen filled with friends and good food.

When I sat down, Melody tapped on her iced tea glass with a spoon. "I have an announcement," she said. "This morning I called Teresa Parra. She's Angel's goddaughter and she's coming over this afternoon to talk with Lila about possibly staying with her until she's better."

Lila clapped her hands. Her eyes sparkled. "She's the nursing student you told me about, Emma, and she sounds absolutely delightful," she said.

I felt a lightness descend on me, a normalcy that I hadn't felt in weeks. "That's great news," I said. "What's her schedule?"

Angel piped in. "She is available, Senora. She has been looking for work, and a place to live for the upcoming school year. If she and the senora like each other and make the agreement, she can start in two days."

Inwardly, I did a little happy dance. One problem out of the way. If Angel vouched for Teresa, then Teresa was the one.

After lunch, I leashed Winston and took him for a walk up the road beyond the Westerly grounds. I needed to be alone for a while, and Winston provided the right combination of enthusiastic but undemanding company. As we walked, I made a quick call to Florian and asked him to please come out to Lila's tonight to spend the night. I told him about the body in the settee, and how Lila's house no longer felt like a safe place.

"Come by yourself," I told him. "This is not going to be a night to socialize."

He agreed to show up about seven. "Perfect," I said. "Come prepared." Not that I needed to tell him. I knew Florian knew what I meant.

By the time Winston and I concluded our walk, Teresa was just leaving from her meeting with Lila—and Angel and Melody. Tall and angular, Teresa exuded the confidence of someone who could run a small country. She greeted me with a firm handshake. She was in her third year of nursing school, which was perfect should Lila need any on-the-spot medical help. And it appeared the meeting had gone well.

Once she departed, I sidled up to Lila. "I want you to call the daughters and ask them to come out tonight a little after seven," I said. "Stephanie, too. Before I leave, I think we all should have a conversation about what's next, and I'm only too happy to moderate."

Lila gave me a confused look. "Is it about the will?" she asked.

"It's about a lot of things, Lila. I don't want to take off and leave you up there at the house without us getting a few things out on the table. It'll be good for everyone to clear the air."

Actually, I didn't have a clue what we'd talk about—yet. But I'd think of something. I wasn't going to leave Lila up there, as prey to whomever was out and about doing weird things like shooting out windows and sticking dead bodies in settees. And I didn't want some weirdo scaring off the new help. Seeing the three sisters face-to-face promised to be an enlightening, if not entertaining event. Maybe once I felt we'd gotten some answers I'd be able to sleep comfortably until I returned to Portland. And then again, maybe not. It was worth a try.

A little after three I got a call from Detective Haymore informing me it was safe to return Lila to her home. "Any surprises?" I asked, hoping against hope that he'd tell me something. I'd been so good, so cooperative, after all.

Haymore was not to be teased out of anything. "Not that I can talk about, Ms. Golden, as you surely know after all the quality time we've spent together in the last two weeks."

It was the first time since I'd met him that I'd gotten a glimpse of humor out of the man—wry humor. Perhaps there was hope. "I have a confession to make," I told him. "Lila and I are going to have a talk with her three daughters tonight about her will and some other matters. You're not invited."

"Humph," was all he had to say.

"Of course, should anything turn up that affects the case you're working on, I'll certainly give you a ring."

"I would expect nothing less from you, Ms. Golden." He disconnected.

Lila and I got busy collecting our things for the drive back to her house. As usual, Angel had packaged up some odds and ends from the refrigerator so that we wouldn't have to cook dinner. I was particularly grateful, since I'd been the designated meal planner and cook for nearly a week. On top of that, my nerves were shot.

Melody walked with us to the car, helped Lila in, and then joined me at the drivers' side. "I know you're up to something," she said. "Just remember, you're dealing with a nest of vipers."

Didn't I know it. "That's why I invited Florian out to spend the night," I said. "After finding that body, I am not sleeping in that house without protection. Frankly, I'm concerned for Lila's safety. I'm sure Florian can handle a few snakes."

Melody gave me a big hug. "Just be careful, she said.

Back at the house, Lila headed for her bedroom. "Did you get hold of the girls?" I asked as she was settling in for a nap.

Lila removed her wig and placed it on the night stand. "Yes, yes. Stephanie is grumpy, as usual, but said she'd be here. The other two sounded excited. They probably think I'm going to give them something—like a big pile of money."

At least they're predictable, I thought. I put Angel's food offerings in the refrigerator, then tiptoed down the hall for a little nap of my own. I climbed onto the bed with my notebook and began writing a brief outline for our meeting. By the time I had that figured out, it was nearly six. I went into the bathroom, splashed my face with cold water and dried off. Then, I commenced applying makeup. I don't wear a lot of makeup, but there are times in a girl's life when nothing short of full war paint will get the job done. This was one of those times!

I roused Lila from her rest and directed her to the bathroom to put on her own war paint. Meanwhile, I assembled the items Angel had sent home with us. We enjoyed a light but quiet supper. Neither of us felt like talking. Lila looked beautiful, but very tense. And then it was seven o'clock. Showtime.

CHAPTER 21

Florian was the first to arrive, as I had intended. He carried his duffel down the hall to the room next to mine. He unpacked a few things and tucked a small pistol (yes, it was Melody's baby Glock) into the back of his jeans. I always wondered how people managed to stuff guns where they do without shooting their parts off, but one never reads about it in the newspaper, so it probably doesn't happen a statistically significant number of times. Obviously, Florian knew enough about guns to keep things from being shot off.

Once the gun was secured, he said, "So, darling, is this what you Yanks call a come-to- Jesus meeting?"

I nodded with approval. "If you like. I'm going home Tuesday, and I want to make certain Lila is going to be safe up here once I leave," I said. "Those girls have been up to something, and we need to get everything out on the table and make certain they're not involved in all of this weirdness."

Florian shrugged. "And if not them, who? Those blokes from Nevada?"

We headed back toward the living room. "Possibly," I said. "By now my friends at the sheriff's office no doubt have talked to the FBI. They're still in custody. But remember, they still claim they were looking for Weatherman, which puts the likelihood of them killing him way out there."

"So what do you want me to do?" Florian said.

"Make yourself invisible. Read the paper, watch from the fringes. Listen. Above all, listen to everything these women have to say."

We found Lila pacing the living room doing a horrible job of hiding her nerves. A residual odor lingered in the air, but for the most part all evidence of Max Weatherman' horrible end were long gone. I glanced at my watch. Seven-fifteen. They should be here any minute now. I put on water for tea and made a pot of decaf. If nobody else wanted it, I sure as hell did.

Florian treated himself to three fingers of Lila's best of scotch. "Lila, darling," he said. "You must stop this pacing or we'll all be a bundle of nerves."

Lila stopped abruptly. "I'm sorry."

Florian took Lila by the arm and led her to the sofa. "Not to worry, darling. But come sit with me. Maybe a little sip of something would calm you a bit, yes?" He sat down next to her.

He raised his eyebrows at me to bring on the medicine, but Lila demurred. "I'm not supposed to drink," she said. "It's not a good idea."

"Well, then, just sit down here, luv. The world isn't going to end."

How did he know? And I'm the one who needed the scotch since I'd called this stupid meeting. I knew it wouldn't work for me either. I took a couple of deep breaths and poured myself a cup of fresh decaf. Then I took Lila a cup of some herbal tea of the calming persuasion.

Stephanie was the first to arrive. She walked in through the front door without knocking, and came into the center of the living room. She looked at all of us. She'd come straight from work from the looks of her. Her clothes were splotched with red wine. More wine had stained her calves. Her hair was its usual greasy mess. "Howdy," she said without enthusiasm.

Lila rose from the sofa and said, "Come in, sweetheart. Thank you for coming. Have a seat. Your sisters aren't here yet." Her nervousness was palpable.

Stephanie allowed herself to be hugged. "What's this about?" she said.

Lila wrung her hands and fluttered. "Come and have a seat, dear." She pulled out a chair at the dining room table. "We can talk about it when everyone is here."

Florian remained in his corner and said nary a word. He was sipping his scotch and seemed to be much occupied with a newspaper. Stephanie, if she even noticed he was there, never gave him a glance.

I offered her a cup of decaf. Instead, she pulled a bottle of pinot noir out of the tote bag she carried, and began opening it with a corkscrew, also from the bag. I provided her a wineglass while Lila continued to flutter. "Have a seat, Lila," I said. She was driving me nuts. "I'll just bring your tea over." In two days, I told myself, I would be at home and waiting on myself. The day could not come soon enough.

The living room door opened again and Morgan came in, pretty and plump and rarin' to sell real estate. She was dressed in a tank top, pink shrug sweater, a floral print skirt, and ridiculously high heels, and carried a large leather folder lest anyone think she was going to a party rather than doing business.

Hot on her heels was Regan, wearing a power suit and carrying the briefcase. Her stern demeanor gave us all notice that nonsense would not be tolerated. From his corner in the living room, Florian watched us over his newspaper as everyone said hello and got seated at the table. I offered coffee, tea, and wine. The sisters opted for wine.

Then Regan noticed. Florian. "What's he doing here?" she said.

Lila started to stay something, but I butted in. "He's just here to spend the night," I said. The sisters looked at me, is if trying to imagine us as a couple. "Don't worry, he won't bother you." Florian took another sip of scotch and retreated behind the newspaper.

I was fairly certain the girls would forget about him soon, as Lila was about to drop the proverbial bomb. I'd coached her in opening the meeting. Once things got rolling, we'd just have to wing it, but getting started was the important thing for now.

With everyone seated, beverages in front of them, Lila announced, "We're ready to get started. Thanks, girls, for taking the time to come tonight. I know it's a lot to ask for you to drive clear out here in the evening, but there are things that need to be discussed."

Morgan and Stephanie squirmed in their seats as if uncomfortable with what might come next. Regan sat erect, her eyes on her mother, unblinking and cold as a reptile's. I set a legal pad and pen on the table in front of me so I could take notes. Not to be outdone, Regan dug in her briefcase for her own legal pad.

Stephanie's anxiety could no longer be contained. "Mom, are you going to sell the winery?" she asked.

Lila looked abashed. "Your mother isn't planning to sell the winery at this point," I said. "What we're here for is to have a past-due discussion about the family business."

That gave Lila the time she needed to collect herself. "Yes," she said. "Over the last week, two of you have approached me with your ideas as to the disposition of the winery since your father's death. First of all, I want to assure everyone that it is not my intention to sell the winery. That is non-negotiable. Stephanie, you do a fine job of winemaking and managing the winery. It's your passion, and your source of livelihood. As long as someone in the family is able to be involved and the winery is doing well, I see no reason to even consider selling. It is increasing in value every day we're here, which is good for all of us in the short run."

I glanced around the table. Stephanie—still tense. Morgan—nonplussed. Regan—stone faced. We had just covered the short run. And, as the noted British economist John Maynard Keynes once observed, we're all dead in the long run.

Which segued us nicely into the second topic, the will. My eyes wandered to Florian, in his corner with the newspaper blocking my view of his face. His glass was empty, and for all I knew he could be sleeping back there.

Lila picked up the ball again. "I know that you, Morgan and Regan, have expressed concern about my role in the winery since your dad's death. As a result of what I have felt to be excessive pressure from the two of you to sell the estate, I have amended my will.

Very simply, I have fixed it to remove any possibility for conflict of interest."

Well, that got their attention. Morgan's mouth opened and closed like a fish. Stephanie looked back and forth between her two sisters with obvious astonishment. Regan leaned forward in Lila's direction. "Mother, as I've mentioned several times, we've been very concerned about you," she said. "You've been very ill, and are undergoing chemotherapy. You live in this huge house and it's an hour's drive for either Morgan or I to get out here, should you need help. We were only suggesting these changes so that you'd have fewer worries and more accessibility to health care and the services you'll need once you've finished treatment."

"I understand your concern completely," Lila said. How she could say this with a straight face I'll never know. Obviously Regan believed her own bull-puckie. I looked at Stephanie. Her faced had turned ashen and her eyes were fixed on Regan. Lila continued, "That is why I've decided to re-evaluate my will and take some matters out of the hands of anyone who might have an emotional attachment. I called this meeting to inform you that I've changed my will and named Emma as my executor. Dan Wyatt, who is well respected in the Portland financial community, will continue to manage all our investments. In the event of my death, they will be managed under

Emma's supervision. There may be further changes, but for now that is where we are."

She had to stop talking. Regan was on her feet. "How can you do this?" she demanded. "With all due respect, Emma is *not* family. I don't even know what she's doing out here, besides trying to get her hands on our money. And you just gave her the key!"

Lila held up her hands and motioned Regan to sit. "Emma is well vetted," she said. "Besides, she's the one who came out here when I needed help and you all were too busy. I know you're not working at the moment, Regan. Why couldn't you have come out for a couple nights?"

Everyone turned their attention to Regan and her suddenly surprised expression.

"You're not working?" Stephanie said.

"Oh my God, what happened?" said Morgan. I was astonished that she didn't know. Her big sister's shadow, and all that.

Regan glared at her mother briefly, then said, "Since you already know, Mother, why don't you tell us why Regan isn't working."

Lila pursed her lips. "I learned that you have been disbarred, Regan. You've never mentioned it, even though it happened several weeks ago. Other than that, I know nothing."

"It's all a big mistake," Regan said. "I'm going to appeal the decision, so let's just forget about singling me out for negative attention."

Stephanie and Morgan exchanged a look. Lila plunged forward. "Since James died, it's been very difficult for me to be in this house, especially alone. So, Morgan? Summer break? I know realtors can make their schedules flex when they need to. Why haven't you offered to help me?"

Morgan piped in, "What about Stephanie? She's already out here. Why couldn't she stay here? Why does it always have to be *us*? It's been that way since we were kids."

Well, boo hoo, Morgan. I found myself praying for patience. Sometimes I was grateful my family consisted of just me and a very distant daughter. It saved one a lot of scenes, not to mention misery.

Lila took in the bunch of them. What she saw seemed to make her more tired than usual. Her shoulders sagged. "None of you have stepped up to help. The only thing I've heard from Morgan and Regan is clamoring for me to sell the estate. It's made me terribly nervous, and that's why I changed the will," she said. "As long as Stephanie is able, she continues to run the winery. It is not going to be sold until circumstances change, and then I will take another look at things."

She paused to take a sip of tea. I glanced at my watch. Past Lila's bedtime. "In the event that I am unable, or am not here to make decisions, Emma will make those decisions for me. I trust she will carry out my wishes to the best of her ability for the benefit of all three of you."

Again Regan was on her feet. "You can't do that!" She practically shouted it.

Lila assessed her calmly. "Well, my dear, I already have."

Morgan started to cry. Stephanie looked squarely at Regan. "You told me that Dad wanted to sell the winery because Mom was sick. Did you tell me the truth?"

Regan sat. Her face registered mild alarm. "We don't need to be talking about that now," she said.

"Yes we do," said Stephanie. "I believed you. That's why—." She stopped and put her hand over her mouth.

Now we were getting somewhere. "Why what, Stephanie?" I asked.

"Nothing. Don't put words in my mouth," she snapped.

I watched as Florian stirred behind the newspaper. I noticed the girls' glasses were empty and I filled them with more wine. Hopefully, that would keep them talking.

Regan rose from her seat a third time. "Well, I think I've heard about enough of this." Her voice dripped sarcasm. "I drove out here to be insulted? I don't appreciate that, Mother. Next time send me an e-mail." She picked up her briefcase and stuffed the legal pad into it.

Morgan began digging in her excessive handbag, as if she thought she was going to go too. She had quit crying but her face was red and blotchy and she continued to snivel. Stephanie reached for her wine, took a sip, and regarded the rest of us warily, if a bit smugly. As of tonight, she still had a job that wouldn't be threatened any time soon. She sat back and stretched out her legs.

"Not so fast," I said to Regan. "Stick around. We still have some things to discuss, and they're pretty important." To wit: "Does anyone notice anything missing from this room?"

Everyone looked around, including Lila. The girls shrugged and looked at each other. Not Lila. "Goodness sakes," she exclaimed. "I believe my lovely antique settee is missing. I wonder where it might have gone. Does anyone have any ideas?"

One of the daughters squeaked. I think it was Stephanie. Regan glowered at me—as if I'd perhaps taken the thing. Morgan recommenced oozing tears. I swear to God, I was sick of the lot of them.

"Nobody. Has. Any. Idea?" Lila said. "Well, that's really something. Why, just this morning Emma opened the settee. And guess what she found? A dead, rotting body. And none of you knows anything about it?"

I had to hand it to her. She had done the Pissed-Off Mom thing before. She just took over and ran with it. Morgan began sobbing loudly.

Lila continued without acknowledging her middle daughter. "After we found the body, we called the police. A forensics team was in my house all day. It terrifies me to think that one of you, or all of you, may have murdered someone in this house. Did you really think a bag of lime was going to hide the smell of rotting human flesh forever? I want to know what's going on, right now, before the police come out again. Because once they get here, we're done talking."

Stephanie was the first to speak. "Dad was going to sell him the winery," she said. "Max Weatherman wanted to buy the winery, and Dad was going to sell it to him."

Lila looked at her youngest in disbelief. "Nonsense," she said. "Where on earth did you get that idea?"

Stephanie ran a hand through her greasy hair. "Regan told me. She'd heard them talking, and Dad was just hanging on waiting for the best price, and then he was going to sell."

Regan looked calmly at Stephanie, her reptilian expression unchanged. Meanwhile, Morgan dabbed at her eyes. She had shut up so that she could hear what was going on. Her face registered fear as she looked from Stephanie to Regan and back again.

Lila wasn't buying it. She leaned toward Stephanie and said, "Did it occur to you to ask your father about this? Or me? Because if he was talking about selling the winery, I would have been in on it and so would you. All of you. I am as much of an owner as he was. When there were decisions to be made about the winery, we always talked about every detail."

Stephanie looked shocked—as if such a possibility had never occurred to her.

Lila observed her sadly. "Did you talk to anyone about this besides Regan? Your dad? Anyone? You didn't want to ask?"

Tears welled up in Stephanie's eyes. "No. I didn't. It was just between us. I was pretty confused. I've been having a hard time lately."

"Good God, Stephanie! You were involved in killing a man in my house because you were having a hard time? Tell me I'm imagining this!"

Stephanie pitched forward and hid her face in her crossed arms. Her body heaved noiselessly as if she, too, was crying.

Regan could not stay seated. "This is just too ridiculous, all these accusations and fantasies. I have no idea what Stephanie is talking about, and I've had enough this bullshit. I'm going home."

Stephanie raised her head from her arms and stared at her sister in blotchy-faced horror.

At last, from the corner, Florian Craig put down his newspaper and unfolded from his chair. By that point, everyone had forgotten about him including me. He walked across the room and pointed at Regan. "You sit down, young lady. Nobody is going anywhere until we get to the bottom of this." Regan sat.

Florian advanced to the liquor cabinet and refilled his scotch. Then he sat at the table's remaining chair. He reached across the table and gently squeezed Stephanie's hand as if they knew each other well. As if he understood things no one else could cipher. And then he said, "Now, Stephanie darling, please finish your story."

CHAPTER 22

Unlike the rest of us, Florian was the picture of serenity—relaxed, composed, even mildly bored. But I, who know him, noticed the coldness of his dark eyes and the tightness at the corners of his mouth.

Stephanie looked up and into his eyes. She appeared to be confused and frightened. "There's not much to tell," she said. "Regan told me that Max Weatherman was coming to the house to meet with Mom about selling the winery. But then she reminded me about Mom's chemo. Her friend Callie Barton was driving her to chemo that day—I remember Regan telling me that. So Mom couldn't meet with Weatherman. Regan said I should handle it since I was the one who was in charge of the winery anyway."

Florian again reached across the table and patted her on the hand. "Very good, Stephanie. And you were angry, weren't you?" He asked matter-of-factly as if her anger was understandable.

Stephanie's eyes flashed. "I was furious! The balls! I mean, him coming up here just a few days after Dad died to continue putting pressure on Mom. And Mom was having such a hard time since Dad was killed. I felt really bad about it."

Florian didn't miss a beat. "Bad about what, Stephanie darling?"

In a flash, Stephanie's expression changed from angry to sad. "Well, Dad, of course. I've had a chance to think about it. I believe it was all a huge mistake and that I over-reacted. But at the time it seemed reasonable. Somebody had to stop him from selling, didn't they?" She looked into Florian's eyes, asking for answers.

Florian held up his hands. "Wait, wait, wait, darling. I'm a little confused. Are we talking about your father now, or Max Weatherman?"

We all watched silently. And as we watched, I realized that Stephanie's story had taken an unexpected turn as she seemed to teeter between fantasy and reality. "Why, Dad, of course," she said. "He was going to sell the winery."

"But, wait," Florian said again. "They had that fight at the Salmon Bake, remember? Your dad punched Weatherman in the nose, and then Weatherman landed a good one and knocked your dad on his bum. You were there, yes?"

Stephanie looked earnestly at Florian. "No, I don't think I remember the fight. I was somewhere else."

"Where did you go, Stephanie? This is important, darling," Florian persisted.

"I'd left something in the car," she said. "I had to go to my car."

Sweet Jesus, I thought. Everyone was wandering every which way that night. Hadn't the police questioned her? And if they did, how could she get past them when I came within an inch of being arrested for murder? There was no explaining it.

Stephanie still looked confused—as if she could barely remember a night just over two weeks ago. "Well, I'd left Mom's knife in the car. Her chef's knife."

Florian sounded infinitely kind, infinitely patient. "And why did you have your mom's chef knife, Stephanie, luv?" he asked.

Stephanie shook her head sadly. "Someone had to stop Dad. He was going to sell the winery."

There was a moment of dead silence at the table. Nobody moved. I eased out a breath I'd been holding for who knows how long. Stephanie. She'd killed her father.

Regan could no longer contain herself. "No!" she shouted. "Stephanie! I'm advising you. You need to stop talking now!"

It broke the spell. Stephanie turned on her. "Just shut up," she said. "Now you say no, but then it was yes. We have to do something. We have to stop him. It's all you could talk about. We, we, we! There was no end to it. So I took care of it. And now I'm not even sure I did the right thing. But yes, I did stab him. I waited for him out to the porta-potties because I knew he had to pass them to get to his car. And I caught him just as he was coming out. He didn't know what hit him. I mean, I'm absolutely sure he didn't feel anything. I was very fast."

She seemed very calm when she looked at Lila. "Mom, tell me this," she said. "Were you and Dad really going to sell the winery to Max Weatherman?"

Lila sighed. Her face registered a profound sadness. "No, sweetheart. We were not going to sell the winery. No. We'd never even considered it."

Florian had one last question. "And who shot at us the other night?" he asked. He looked at all three of the daughters.

Stephanie was staring at Regan and Morgan. Regan sat tight-lipped. Morgan finally spoke. "We did," she said. "We didn't want to hurt anyone. We just wanted to scare you."

After that, things moved quickly. Florian kept an eye on everyone at the table. The daughters all began shouting accusations at each other. I hot-footed it down the hall to my bedroom, where I called Haymore and Jeffers and told them to get up here right away. We had learned the murderer's identity, she was with us, and they needed to take over.

When I returned to the dining room, an agitated Stephanie was explaining to Florian how she had killed Max Weatherman—but this time it was the ten-inch chef's knife because the eight-inch one, which, she explained was actually a nicer size, was no longer available.

Weatherman had been lured up to the house by none other than Regan herself, who told him that Lila was ready to sell the winery. He had been admitted by Regan, who then informed him Lila wasn't at home and that she, representing the family, was designated to negotiate with him. As they stood in the living room talking about the potential sale, Stephanie stabbed him from behind. Between the two of them, they were able to lift Weatherman's dead weight into the settee and clean up a huge quantity of blood before Lila returned some time later from her chemotherapy. We later learned that the forensic team's analysis of the wood floor around the settee revealed evidence of the blood and blood spattering that confirmed this.

Shortly after Haymore and Jeffers arrived with a backup unit, they summoned another car to take Stephanie to the Yamhill County Jail. She was to be isolated and on suicide watch, and to undergo complete physical and psychiatric evaluations during the coming days.

After segregating and talking with the rest of us, they also took Morgan and Regan to the jail for further questioning. A couple hours later, they were finished with us and we were left to our own devices.

It was after midnight when Lila crawled off to bed, a broken woman. In a matter of a few hours, her family had been destroyed before her very eyes.

Florian and I sat up for a long time, both of us too emotionally drained to even think about retiring. Sometimes we talked about the day's events. Sometimes we talked about some of the fun things we'd done together in the past at wine judging's in various parts of the country. Sometimes we just sat there for long periods of silence. For me, at least, the idea of going off to bed alone with my thoughts, was too much to bear.

CHAPTER 23

Two weeks later, at Portland International Airport, Melody, Cat, and I sat in a restaurant eating breakfast with Florian Craig. He was returning to New York. Cat, wearing a rather ostentatious diamond engagement ring, had just listed her house in Lower Hillsdale Heights, and was planning to join Florian in Manhattan as soon as it sold. Meanwhile, we were informed, there would be several cross-country visits. I was very happy that something besides murder had come to pass as a result of that night at the IPNC Salmon Bake.

Cat and Florian were busy planning an October wedding with reception at the Westerly, as well as a gala party to follow in New York City. We laughed and talked about past and future good times, weddings, and food. We avoided the topic that still haunted me every time the four of us were together.

Regan, Morgan, and Stephanie Ryder all had been indicted in the deaths of James Ryder and Max Weatherman. All were lawyered up, and it was thought that Stephanie's attorney would seek a not guilty by reason of insanity defense. There was no question that Stephanie had killed both men. She'd flat out admitted it to the authorities after they read her her rights. But many questions still surrounded her actions. Her inability to cope with the most basic human relations, her gullibility, and her naiveté—all raised flags with the mental health professionals who had talked with her. What was going with her would not be revealed for some time.

Meanwhile, from what I could tell, both of the older sisters were involved up to their eyeballs in planning the murders, and in talking Stephanie into actually doing the dirty work. How it would all play out would depend on juries of our finest citizens.

I'd returned home from Yamhill County in a saddened state. Lila somehow managed to keep going. She's a very strong woman. She's had to be. She got on well with her new caregiver, Teresa. She followed her medical protocol and slept a lot. She coped. I'd been out a couple of times to visit her and check on things, and she told me that, awful as it was, it was good to have closure on James's death. As far as having relationships with her daughters, she'd come to terms with those difficulties long ago.

I also found myself being drawn back into Melody's life. I'd stop by the Westerly for a dip in the pool after my visits with Lila, and enjoyed my visits with Melody, Angel, and Winston. Dan returned from Alaska, and every time he saw me I left the house laden with fresh garden vegetables and frozen salmon and halibut.

While I'd soon have to cope with Cat moving away from Portland, I was happy for her. I'd miss her and all the activities we'd shared, particularly in the years since I'd moved back to the city, but she deserved the best life had to offer her. I only hoped this was it.

Later that night found me scribbling in my journal in my cozy home in Lower Hillsdale Heights. There was even more to report. I'd just learned that very afternoon that I would be hired for a half-time job at a local theatre where I'd work with their publicity director on press releases and events planning. I was thrilled beyond measure.

Also that day I'd received a letter from Lila—such a lovely, old-fashioned thing in this digital age. She informed me that in light of recent developments she was considering putting the Ryder Estate on the market. With cancer she faced an uncertain future. Her three daughters were felons. Her husband was dead. And she was tired. What was left for her out there? It was time to let go and move on to the next stage of her life.

She thanked me effusively for my service to her and expressed gratitude for our developing friendship. If she moved into Portland, she said, we'd see each other more often. She enclosed a generous check to cover my time spent helping her.

"Change is constant," she said at the conclusion of her brief letter. To which I say, Amen.

ACKNOWLEDGEMENTS

When a person writes a book, the actual creation of the story certainly is the biggest part. However, as an indie author, it is more than just the writing of the book. I also oversee the production of the book at all levels and work with a great many people to bring it to fruition. I feel a great deal of gratitude to all the people who helped me at all stages during the creation and production of *The Man Who Wasn't There*.

My deepest thanks to Aaron Yeagle, a friend and associate who is responsible for the design and functioning of my web site, www.judynedry.com. He speaks a language I cannot comprehend, and although I am responsible for most of the copy, he's the guru who keeps things up to date and looking good. Aaron also understands things like search engine optimization (another foreign language to me), and performs many invisible functions in areas unknown to me. For this book, Aaron is responsible for cover design as well. Kudos, my friend!

A huge thank you to McMinnville photographer Doreen Wynja, who provided the beautiful cover image taken of Kiff Vineyard outside McMinnville. I've known Doreen for years, and she has built a formidable portfolio of images from wineries and vineyards in the Pacific Northwest and beyond. I am glad we could work together once again.

Thanks to Jennifer King for all the time and coaching you spent to create my cover portrait.

And a round of applause for my readers: Linda Baldwin, Linda Eguchi, Rebecca Gabriel, Lynn Greenwood, Judy Heller, JoAnn Herrigel, Morgan Kearns, Jennifer King, Karen Knight, Toni Morgan, Janet Nedry, Wynne Peterson-Nedry, and Carol Wire. You beautiful women have the most wonderful and constructive ways of getting me back on track. You correct my typos and go through everything with a fine-tooth comb. As a result, both the book and I benefit tremendously. In short, you're the greatest!

A LETTER TO MY READERS

To my fabulous readers,

Thank you for your support in reading Book 3 of the Emma Golden Mystery Series, *The Man Who Wasn't There*. I hope you enjoyed the book and will seek out the previous books in the series.

I encourage interaction with my readers, and would love to hear from you. Whether you loved or hated the book, you may send your comments to me personally at authorjudynedry@yahoo.com. You're invited to visit my website, www.judynedry.com, where you may subscribe to the newsletter/blog, get all the latest news on book signings and events, and be the first to learn what is next in Emma Golden's world. There also is space for your comments.

Finally, I ask your support as a reviewer. It's a very tough market for fiction writers, particularly indie fiction writers. You readers have the power now to make or break *The Man Who Wasn't There*. Like it or not, you, gentle readers are my marketing team. If you have the time, ***please visit Amazon.com or Goodreads and leave a short review***. Just a rating and a couple sentences is really all that is needed—although please write more if you like.

What else can you do? "Like" Emma Golden Mysteries on Facebook. Invite me to do a reading/signing at your book group (Portland area only). Ask your library to order the book. Ask your local bookstore to stock the book. And above all, talk about the book. It is amazing how many new Emma Golden fans come to me through word-of-mouth.

Thanks for everything. I truly hope to meet you in person one day.

– Judy Nedry